AS LONG AS I HAVE YOU

London Sullivans 1

Bella Andre

AS LONG AS I HAVE YOU
London Sullivans 1
© 2019 Bella Andre

Sign up for Bella's New Release Newsletter
www.BellaAndre.com/newsletter
bella@bellaandre.com
www.BellaAndre.com
Bella on Twitter: @bellaandre
Bella on Facebook: facebook.com/bellaandrefans

All Mari Everett's life, she's had two secret dreams: to own a bookstore and to reunite with her long-lost father. But when he passes away unexpectedly, and she inherits his home and business, the only way she can learn about his life—and why he abandoned her when she was three and never came back—is by leaving California to take over his bookstore in London.

Owen Sullivan lives and works on Elderflower Island, a close-knit London community where it's impossible to keep a secret. It turns out, however, that Charlie Forsythe kept his daughter a secret from everyone for nearly thirty years. When Mari comes to London, Owen immediately falls for her. He's never met a woman so intelligent, determined, and honest. Not to mention so beautiful that she takes his breath away.

Soon, everyone on the island—including Owen's four siblings, his parents, and even his grandmother—is pitching in to give the bookstore a fresh start. But as insatiable passion develops into love, will Mari and Owen be able to grab hold of their fresh start? Or will their pasts continue to cast a dark shadow over their chance at a brilliant future together in London?

A note from Bella

I love to travel, and whenever I visit a beautiful new place, I always find myself storing scents, experiences, and images in my mind so that I can share them with readers. As I write about somewhere I've been—Napa Valley, California; Pike Place Market, Seattle; Hart Island, New York; Mount Desert Island, Maine—I can't help but want to hop in a car or plane and experience their beauty again.

I first visited England when I was a teenager, on a trip with my parents to learn about Shakespeare in Stratford-upon-Avon, and also to visit my mother's brother and sister, who both live in London. I went a second time in college while on a six-month transfer program in Paris. Since then, I've lost track of how many times I have been back to England. All I know is that I'm constantly wishing I could be there again. The sooner the better!

I love everything about Great Britain—the landscape, the history, the traditions, the accents. I can happily spend hours exploring museums and castles and winding cobblestone streets.

As Long As I Have You is my love letter to London—and to the newest branch of the Sullivan family. I hope you fall as much in love with the London Sullivans as I already have.

Happy reading,
Bella Andre

P.S. While Elderflower Island is my own fictional creation, I have been heavily inspired by Eel Pie Island in southwest London, along with the London Borough of Richmond upon Thames. For those of you who know the area well, thank you for allowing this American writer the license to embellish a few major details here and there throughout my books.

P.P.S. More stories about the London Sullivans are coming soon! Please be sure to sign up for my newsletter (BellaAndre.com/newsletter) so that you don't miss out on any new book announcements.

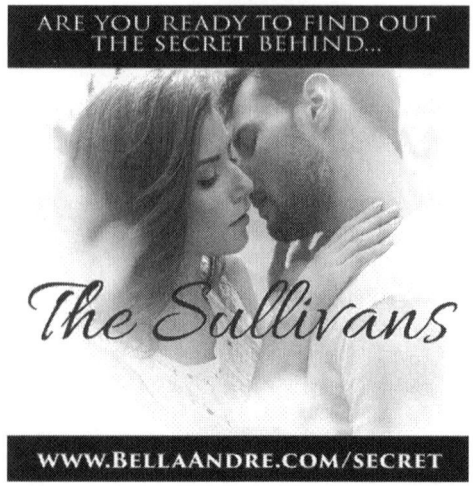

CHAPTER ONE

Mari Everett didn't have time to pop into the bookstore during her lunch hour, but as always, she couldn't resist looking in the window. Bookstores were her catnip.

Her brother, Carson—stepbrother, technically—laughed as she paused at the front door. "Go on in, you know you want to."

"I can go another day. After all, I never know the next time I'll get to have lunch with you." Carson practically lived on a plane lately as he worked to build his tech company.

"We can spare five minutes for you to get your bookstore fix and still have time to eat before your budget review meeting." He scowled through the words *budget review*. "Remind me again why you work at an accounting firm rather than owning a place like this?"

"I'm great with numbers, and I really like helping people get their financial lives in order," Mari reminded her brother.

"So it has nothing to do with the fact that Mom would totally freak out if you ran a bookstore?"

Mari knew better than to try to deny it, not when Carson knew her—and their mother—better than anyone. "It certainly wouldn't be her profession of choice for me."

It was no secret to either of them that, while Donna Everett seemed so tough and strong on the outside, within their mother lay a deep fragility and vulnerability due to the circumstances of her first marriage to Mari's birth father. Mari remembered how her mother used to cry and cry all those years ago. Even now, Donna could still fall into a funk if something triggered a memory from the past.

"All I'm saying," Carson added, "is that from my perspective, you've never looked anywhere near as happy in your cubicle crunching numbers as you do when you're in a bookstore." He reached past her to open the door. "After you."

Not wanting to get into yet another debate about her life choices, Mari simply said, "Promise to yank me out after five minutes."

Once inside, she took a deep breath. *Ahhh.*

She loved the smell of books, both old and new. Loved the way they looked on the shelves, some colorful and fun, others serious and restrained. Loved how they felt in her hands, everything from glossy hardcovers to purse-sized paperbacks. Most of all, she loved feeling like she could learn everything, could become absolutely anything, all because of books.

There was a bigger, newer bookstore a few blocks away, and she'd spent many happy hours there over the years. But this store, with its antique shelves, old rugs over an even older wood floor, velvet armchairs, and a snuffling bulldog lounging on the floor by the register—this was her favorite place in Santa Monica.

Frankly, she was amazed a store like this could thrive in a Southern California city where people seemed interested only in the new and flashy. The owner, Nils, a sixtysomething Norwegian man with an encyclopedic knowledge of authors, had carved out his own special niche in the middle of Beach Town, USA. The cozy, somewhat cluttered store was always a welcome respite from the blazing sun.

When Mari was in Nils's store, she could pretend she lived somewhere that didn't have only one season. A city filled with history and stories that went back more than 250 years.

If she tried hard enough, she could almost pretend she was in England…and instead of Nils behind the register, it was her father.

The father she hadn't seen in twenty-nine years.

"Mari, I'm glad you're here." Nils gestured for her to come over to the register. "I found a book I think you'll be very excited about. I was just about to give you a ring, in fact." He rifled through the books haphazardly stacked to his right. "Here it is." He slid a book from the middle of the pile. Miraculously, they didn't all come toppling down.

Mari's heartbeat quickened when she saw the title: *A History of Elderflower Island*.

She wanted to sink into the nearest armchair and devour the information on the faded pages. But she'd have to wait until she was home tonight to feed her secret fascination for the one place on earth that intrigued her more than any other.

Carson saw the title when Nils handed over the book, but apart from a raised eyebrow, he didn't comment. Her brother was the only one in their family who knew that Mari had spent years soaking up information about her birth father's homeland. Thankfully, Carson didn't judge her for it. Just the opposite, in fact—he always encouraged her. Not only to search for information online and in books, but to actually go to London and meet her father face-to-face at the bookstore he owned on Elderflower Island.

But she'd always been so busy, first with school and then work, that there had never been a good time to fly all the way to England. Instead, she enjoyed taking mini-breaks at beach houses with girlfriends and long weekends skiing with her family in the nearby mountains. One day soon, she promised herself, she'd block out time for a longer vacation to explore Europe. Maybe after tax season had come and gone...even though the truth was that tax season pretty much went all year once you factored in all the people and companies that filed for extensions.

Belatedly realizing she hadn't thanked Nils for finding the book, she said, "You're a wonder, always able to find the impossible." She took out her wallet and gave him a twenty.

As he made change, he said, "I got lucky with this one. Looks like there was a bit of a fire sale from a bookstore on the island."

Mari's senses immediately went on red alert. "What do you mean by a *fire sale*? Has something happened to the bookstore?" It had to be her father's. "Or do you think they are simply clearing stock?"

"I wouldn't know for sure without giving them a call. I could do that if you'd like, although with the time difference, they're likely closed for the day."

Carson looked up from a book about World War II that he'd been thumbing through. "Something wrong, Mari?"

Before she could reply, her phone rang.

She was tempted to ignore it, but there was a lot riding on this afternoon's budget meeting at Everett Financial. Mari's assistant, or one of the other staff members, was likely waiting for her to come back from lunch so that she could answer their eleventh-hour questions.

She took her phone out of her bag, but didn't recognize the number on the screen. In fact, the area code wasn't local, but had a +44 in front of a long string of numbers.

The prefix for England was +44.

Oh my God. Could it be…her father?

When Mari was three years old, Charlie Forsythe had left her and her mother, and never made contact again. Had something finally prompted him to reach out to her? Maybe something to do with a fire sale at his bookstore?

Her hand trembled slightly as she accepted the call. "Hello?"

"Hello. My name is Clarence Wencel, and I am a solicitor with Ford, Bixby and Wencel." The man's accent was unmistakably British, as was his use of the word *solicitor* rather than *lawyer*. "I am trying to reach Marina Forsythe."

For as long as Mari could remember, no one had called her Marina Forsythe. After her mother remarried when Mari was four, Mari's surname had been legally changed to Everett. And the name *Forsythe* was never spoken of again.

"Yes, I'm Mari." The words croaked out of her

throat. She turned away from Carson, who was giving her a worried look, and moved to a deserted corner of the store. "How can I help you?" The question was automatic, one she asked co-workers and clients several times a day.

"I'm sorry to have to tell you this news over the telephone, but your father, Charlie Forsythe, has passed away."

Mari's knees gave out. Had there not been a velvet-covered footstool directly behind her, she would have collapsed onto the floor. As it was, shock—and a soul-deep sorrow—had her dropping her phone, the device clattering from her ice-cold hand to the floor.

Carson hurried over and knelt in front of her. "Mari? What's happened?"

She couldn't speak, could only shake her head. Her phone rang again, from the floor.

Finally, she found her voice. "It's my father." *Father* came out on a sob. "He's dead."

"I'm so sorry." Carson's hands covered hers, his touch feeling like the only thing keeping her tethered to the earth. "Would you like for me to talk to whomever is calling?"

Though she was beyond shell-shocked, she shook her head. "I need to do it."

Carson picked up her phone and handed it to her. It had stopped ringing, so she scrolled to her most recent call and hit *Redial*.

"This is Mari. Sorry, I dropped my phone." She swallowed hard, working to keep tears at bay. "Please tell me how he died and anything else I should know."

She listened in silence for several minutes. "Thank you for telling me." Her brain was spinning, but she needed to keep it together, at least until she got off the phone. "I will be in touch once I've decided what to do."

Her limbs felt numb as she put down her phone and closed her eyes. If only she could start the day over. Better yet, the year, so that she could have finally gotten on a plane to England and reached out to her father while he was still alive. Their meeting might have gone badly—but what if it had gone well? What if, despite all the years of separation, they had been able to forge a relationship with each other?

She would never get that chance now.

Carson was sitting beside her, his arm around her shoulders, patiently waiting for her to tell him the rest of what the solicitor had said.

"He had cancer." Her voice didn't sound like her own, too low and scratchy. "He didn't leave a will, but his solicitors were able to determine that I'm his next of kin. He had no other children and no living siblings or parents." She looked into her brother's eyes. "Evidently, this means I'm entitled to all his worldly possessions."

Carson's eyebrows went up. "What have you inherited?"

She had never been so thankful for her brother's steady, nonjudgmental presence. Rather than coddling her, he understood that she needed to lay it all out on the table.

"His bookstore, which has a two-bedroom flat above it. The solicitor said probate will take approximately six weeks, at which point he expects I'll own both the store and the flat outright once all is said and done with death duties. He thinks there will be about five thousand pounds left to support my taking over the bookstore if I choose to."

Carson let the information settle for a few seconds, during which she knew he was turning it over inside his brain, looking at it from all angles. "Whenever you're ready to go to England to check it out, I'll clear my schedule so that I can go with you."

It would be so easy to let him deal with everything. But she knew instinctively that would only lead to more regrets. Plus, she would never forgive herself if Carson's growing business derailed at a crucial moment because he had dropped the ball to take care of her mess.

"Thank you for offering," she said. "But I need to deal with this myself."

"I thought you were going to say that. Just remember that I can always jump on a plane at a moment's notice." He paused before adding, "And whatever happens, don't let Mom change your mind about going to England. I get that her demons are big where your father is concerned, but you've got to do what's right for *you*."

All her life, Mari had been careful to protect her mother from further emotional upheaval. But now that everything had changed in an instant with one short phone call? Though Mari suspected Donna would be devastated to hear Mari's sudden new plans, even that wasn't enough to keep her away anymore.

"I want to see it." No, her feelings were stronger than that. "I *need* to see his bookstore and his home and his island." She couldn't think beyond that yet, couldn't imagine the reality of actually keeping and running his store, or living in the flat upstairs.

"Let me know the date of your flight, and I'll use my frequent-flier miles to get you a lie-flat seat." Carson had encouraged her to travel for years, but she'd never left Southern California. "And I'm thinking you should tear the Band-Aid off as fast as you can with Mom, then give her some time to get over her knee-jerk reaction." One they both knew would be bad.

Though she knew her brother was right, she winced just thinking about it. "First, I need to get back to the office and run the budget meeting."

"You've just learned that your birth father died. Dad will understand if you can't run the meeting."

"I know he will." She loved her stepfather. He had treated her from the beginning as though she was his daughter. "But I can't let him down." Gary Everett had not only given her love, he'd also provided her with every possible opportunity with school and then with her career at his accounting firm. "I can't let him think I'm choosing the father who left me over the one who took me in and stayed."

"He won't think that."

Mari wasn't at all sure that would be the case. The only thing she knew for certain at the moment was that she desperately needed a few hours of normality before she sat down with her parents and gave them the news.

"Come on," she said, forcing herself to her feet. "Let's grab a sandwich before we both have to get back to work." She wasn't the least bit hungry anymore, but she'd force herself to eat something, if only so her brother wouldn't have one more thing to worry about.

They were halfway out the door when Nils rushed over. "You forgot your book."

She slid it into her bag. Now, more than ever, she would need to know the history of Elderflower Island.

CHAPTER TWO

Somehow, Mari made it through the budget meeting. Her cheeks hurt from fake-smiling, and her stomach ached from being twisted in knots all afternoon.

Mari never left work early, but as soon as the meeting concluded, she grabbed her things and slipped out. She needed to be at her best—or as close to it as she could manage—for the upcoming discussion with her parents. That meant heading home to shower off the cold sweat that had covered her upon hearing that Charlie had passed away, putting on a little makeup to give her cheeks some color, then forcing down some food for much-needed energy.

At seven that night, she drove out of the city and into the leafy suburbs off Montana Avenue where her parents lived. The Spanish-style, white stucco house with its half acre of blooming, well-tended garden was the home Mari had lived in nearly all her life. Until she was three, she'd lived with her mother and Charlie in a condominium above a brewpub on Santa Monica's Third Street, in the heart of downtown. But she'd been too young at the time to remember much about her time there.

From the driveway, she could see her mother and stepfather standing together in the kitchen. They looked up through the window, and when they saw her car, they both smiled.

Mari hated knowing that what she was about to tell them would wipe their smiles right off.

Her mother was waiting at the open front door by the time Mari walked up the stone path. "Your timing is perfect if you'd like to join us for dinner, honey. We have more than enough for three."

"I already ate, thanks." She kissed her mother on the cheek. "There's actually something I need to talk about with both you and Dad."

She almost flinched as the word *Dad* left her mouth.

All day, she'd been mourning the loss of the father she'd never really known—and regardless of what Carson had said, she couldn't help feeling that it was a betrayal of the man who had cared for her for the past twenty-nine years with love and care.

Her mother looked at her more closely. "That sounds serious. Is everything okay? Are you feeling sick? Gary didn't mention anything about you not feeling well at the office."

"No, I'm not sick." But things were most definitely

not okay. "We should sit down, and then I'll explain everything."

It was at moments like this when Mari wished she could suggest that her mother and stepfather pour them all a drink. But not only did Donna refuse to drink alcohol, she wouldn't let Gary have one single sip of spirits either. What's more, for as long as Mari could remember, her mother had drummed into her head that her genetics made her a prime candidate for developing a drinking problem.

In the hours that had passed since the solicitor's call, she had gone around and around inside her head to try to find a palatable way to explain her plans to travel to England to see Charlie's flat and bookstore. Unfortunately, she had yet to land on one.

"My birth father—" The immediate look of horror—and fury—on her mother's face made her break off in midsentence.

Mari belatedly realized her first error had been in using the word *father* in reference to him.

Clearing her throat, she began again. "I got a phone call this afternoon. Charlie—"

Her mother cut her off. "Has he contacted you?" Donna turned to Gary. "What did I tell you? I knew there would come a day when he wouldn't leave well enough alone." Donna scowled as she asked Mari, "What did he say?"

For a long moment, all Mari could do was shake her head as she worked to swallow her grief. "Nothing. He's dead."

Her mother gasped, her face going pale as she gripped her husband's hand for support. "How did you find out?"

"A phone call from a solicitor."

She could see both the concern in her stepfather's eyes as he said, "I'm sorry, Mari."

"Well, I'm not." Donna stood, clearly agitated. "That man was a useless, drunk danger to you. I say good riddance."

Though Mari had only vague memories of her father, they were surprisingly good ones. They had played games together—Chutes and Ladders, which he had called Snakes and Ladders; tic-tac-toe, which he had called noughts-and-crosses; and her favorite, conkers.

She had loved exploring the local public garden to look for chestnut trees, then collecting the glossy nuts to find the best conkers for their competition. He would make holes in the conkers so that they could thread a string through each of them. Charlie would then hold his conker steady, dangling it from a string, while she tried with all her might to hit it with hers. Every time she knocked one of his conkers off the string, he would hug her and tell her what a clever little girl she was.

She also remembered his English accent. It didn't much matter what he said—just listening to him speak, or read aloud from one of the dozens of children's books he'd bought her, had been so nice and soothing.

Thinking back to those lovely memories made Mari want to defend Charlie to her mother, however unwise that course of action might be.

Before she could, however, her stepfather asked, "Did the solicitor say anything more?"

"Yes. As I'm his next of kin, his bookstore, flat and savings have now passed to me."

"No!" Donna spun around. "Under no circumstances should you take ownership of anything that was his. There must be a way for you to refuse his estate."

Mari understood why her mother wanted her to do that. But she couldn't bring herself to just up and disavow her father's legacy.

Donna's expression grew even more aghast when Mari's silence indicated that she didn't agree. "You aren't thinking of keeping his store, are you? Do I need to remind you what kind of man he was—and what he did?"

Of course Mari didn't need a reminder, not when she knew the story by heart. Charlie Forsythe had come to California from London, charmed Donna into marrying him, then gotten her pregnant before she realized just how out of control his drinking really was. He was bohemian—he sketched and wrote—but brought in little to no money from a part-time job at a bookstore. They survived because of Donna's job as a secretary at an accounting firm. And then, one day when Mari was three, her father had blacked out when he was supposed to be watching her. Mari had left the apartment and was toddling down busy Third Street when the owner of the downstairs brewpub saw her from the window. Just in time, the man darted out to stop her from crossing the road in front of a delivery truck.

Mari's mother had kicked Charlie out that night, telling him never to come back.

And he never had.

"I know he made mistakes," Mari said, "but I can't make any decisions without going to England."

"I'll save you the trip," her mother said. "Both his store and flat will be a mess, just like he was. In any case, why would you want to own a bookstore—in *England*, of all places—when you have a wonderful job right here at home, with a family who loves you?"

If Mari hadn't already felt guilty, she certainly would have now. The easiest thing would be to bend to her mother's will, to agree that England and everything in it, especially her birth father, were horrible, and turn her back on Charlie's unexpected legacy. But

Mari had always been secretly fascinated by all things British. Especially the southwest corner of London, where her father lived. She'd gone so far as to Google-walk the streets on her computer, trying to imagine what his life was like five thousand miles away—and inevitably wondering what it would have been like to grow up on Elderflower Island instead of in Santa Monica.

"I need to see it for myself." Mari's words were firm, despite the fact that her mother's reaction was even worse than she'd thought it might be. She would never want to hurt Donna, but she couldn't bury her own needs for another moment longer.

Her mother sat, looking shakier than ever. "How long are you planning to be away?"

"I have quite a bit of accrued vacation on the books." Turning to Gary, Mari said, "I'll take the next few weeks to finish my current projects, or pass them into capable hands, before I go." According to the solicitor, she had six weeks until probate was done. Six weeks to prepare herself to finally enter her father's world.

"You have my blessing to do whatever you need to do, Mari."

Donna scowled at her husband, clearly displeased that he would encourage their daughter to pursue anything involving Charlie Forsythe. She turned her attention back to Mari. "You still haven't said how long you'll be gone."

"I don't know yet." Understanding that nothing she said tonight was going to soothe her mother, Mari stood. "Sorry for interrupting your dinner. I'll leave now and let you get to it."

Her mother glowered. "I've completely lost my appetite."

Though Mari wished there was something she could do to bring back her mom's smile, she simply kissed her cheek, gave her stepfather a hug, then saw herself out.

Surprisingly, as she headed to her car, she realized that she felt better than she had all day. One of her biggest dreams was on the verge of coming true. She was finally going to visit her father's home. Though Charlie wouldn't be there to greet her, hopefully she would still find enough clues in his home and business to discover who he had been.

And while she was there, she couldn't help but wonder if she might also discover new things about herself too.

CHAPTER THREE

A business-class, lie-flat seat, courtesy of Carson's air miles, was heaven for the eleven-hour flight from Los Angeles to London. Mari had been able to spread out in the spacious cocoon of her seat, had ordered from the gourmet in-flight menu, and was even given pajamas to change into before sliding beneath the covers. Nonetheless, she'd lain awake, staring at the ceiling of the plane for the rest of the flight, her mind going a million miles an hour.

Yes, she was excited and curious and couldn't wait to see her father's bookstore and Elderflower Island. But at the same time, she was also nervous.

What if she hated it and wanted to return to California immediately? Or what if she loved it and never wanted to leave? What if she took one look at England, at the island, at her father's bookstore and flat, and realized she'd finally found her true home? No question, her mother would never forgive her.

The customs official at the airport couldn't have been more welcoming, all smiles when he asked if she was there for business or a holiday. She didn't know how to answer. Was her trip both? Neither? Finally, she settled on, "My father passed away, and I've come to take care of his affairs."

"I'm very sorry to hear that." He stamped her passport. "I hope you don't have too hard a time of it."

His kindness brought a lump to her throat, one she was still trying to swallow past as she took her luggage off the carousel and went to join the taxi line outside. The air was slightly damp, as though it might start drizzling at any moment. Just the way she'd always imagined England would be.

The solicitor had offered to escort her to the store and flat, but she wanted to be on her own the first time she saw it. After all, who knew how she'd react? Cry or laugh like a loon—either of those emotions felt possible right now.

After the long, sleepless flight, her eyes felt gritty, her head felt like it was stuffed with cotton, and her limbs were strangely rubbery. And yet, from the moment the taxi drove out of London Heathrow, she was mesmerized.

In Southern California, the hills were golden brown nearly year-round. But here the landscape, even on the side of the freeway, was lush and green. So many shades of green, from the fields to the forest, contrasting with the puffy clouds and blue sky peeking out from between them.

The traffic was light, and soon they were taking the exit toward Kew and Richmond. Her heart fluttered as she took in the centuries-old stone and brick buildings, the pubs, the bridge over the river. It was exactly as she'd imagined—even better than what Google had shown her.

Her driver smiled at her in the rearview mirror. "Just last weekend, my wife and I took our grandchildren to Petersham Nurseries. Couldn't find a lovelier spot if you tried."

"I've never been there." But during her research over the years, she'd read plenty about the posh plant store and its onsite restaurant and café.

"American?" When she nodded, he said, "You are in for a treat." He pointed out landmarks: Kew Gardens, the Borough of Richmond, where he claimed several rock stars and actors lived, and then what he told her was his favorite spot of all, Elderflower Island. "I have whiled away many happy hours in the pub while my wife browsed the shops. Including, of course, the best bookshop in London."

For the past twenty minutes, she had been swept into a dream by her surroundings. With a harsh thump, the driver's comment brought her back down to earth.

"That's where I'd like you to drop me." She found it suddenly difficult to catch her breath as the reality of where she was going hit her in the solar plexus. "At the bookstore on the island."

"Are you staying in one of the rooms above the pub?"

"No." In LA she wouldn't have risked giving away personal details, but she couldn't imagine this kindly taxi driver who had just been talking about his grandkids causing her trouble. "I'm staying in the flat above the store."

"Ah, I thought you had a familiar look about you. The owner, Charlie, is a fine fellow. Are you related to him, by any chance?"

Hearing that she resembled her father knocked even more breath from her lungs. "He was my father." Before the driver could comment on her use of the word *was*, she added, "He died last month."

"I'm so sorry to hear that. You have my deepest condolences."

She swallowed hard. "Thank you."

They drove over the bridge to the island, and she almost gasped out loud. Elderflower Island had taken on almost mythical proportions to her over the years.

Amazingly, it did not disappoint.

A large manor house stood regally, if a bit weathered, in the center of the island, looking like something out of a fairy tale, with wrought-iron gates opening to a long drive with a fountain at the center.

Across from the manor house stood another impressive building—the island's concert hall. From her research, she knew it had been a well-respected venue for several decades, jump-starting the careers of many top British bands. Unfortunately, it now seemed to be closed for business.

To the right of the concert hall was a row of picturesque storefronts—a corner grocery, a bakery, a tea shop, a Chinese takeaway, and several boutiques. Each doorway was painted a different color and looked immensely more appealing than the cookie-cutter strip malls she was used to seeing in Santa Monica.

A sign for the Fox & Hound pub jutted out over the street. The whitewashed walls of the pub were surrounded by outdoor seating. Plenty of people were sitting outside enjoying a drink.

Beyond the curve of the road, there was a large boathouse belonging to the island's rowing and sailing club.

And perched directly in front of the river, between the pub and the boathouse, stood her father's bookstore.

Mari's heart just about stopped in her chest as she took it in. The painted sign above the door—*Elderflower Island Books*—was faded. The building, dated 1883, looked plenty faded too.

Belatedly, she realized the driver had already placed

her bags on the sidewalk. Alighting from the taxi, she fumbled for money in her purse. "Thank you. You've been very kind."

He drove off, but she didn't immediately head in. Instead, she stood with her luggage at her feet, staring through the windows of her father's bookstore.

Her bookstore now.

At last, she reached into her purse again and drew out the key the solicitor had mailed to her—an antique skeleton key, forged from heavy metal. The front door was made of wood, and at the center was a hand carving of an open book, a page moving in midair. It was utterly captivating, even under a layer of dust.

This was it. The moment of truth.

On a deep breath, she turned the key in the lock and pushed the door open.

Oh. My. God.

It was absolutely *filthy*.

Books lay everywhere. Not only on the shelves, but also on the floor, on the various chairs and couches, on the windowsills, even on the stairs that she assumed led to the second-floor flat.

Though her father had died only six weeks ago, it didn't look like anyone had been here in months. Certainly not a cleaner, or anything resembling a customer. From her online research, she had assumed the store was thriving. How long had her father been sick? And had there been no one to help him?

Mari had never thought about her father in connection with anyone but her mother and herself, but now that she was finally on the island, she saw how close the cottages, the other businesses, and the manor house were. How could the decline of her father's store possibly have gone unnoticed?

Hopefully, the flat wasn't in as bad a shape as the store. But if it was, she reminded herself that she was more than capable of buying cleaning supplies and giving every inch of the store and flat a good scouring—even if it took several days.

At last, she picked up her bags and carried them inside. Her mother had been horrified when she'd seen how much Mari was taking to England. *"It looks as though you're planning to move there for good!"*

Mari had explained that, regardless of how long she stayed, she needed to be prepared for the unpredictable London weather, which meant jeans and a waterproof jacket and boots, along with lighter clothes and tennis shoes. Her explanation hadn't mollified her mother, however. Now, Mari wished she had packed less so she wouldn't have had so much to lug up the narrow, steep stairs.

As if Donna knew Mari was thinking of her, a text buzzed through to her phone.

Are you there? How was your flight? Is everything okay?

It was four in the morning in California. Mari doubted her mother had gone to sleep, instead waiting up until she heard from her. *I'm here. The flight was good. Don't worry, everything is fine.*

Her mother instantly responded. *Your father and I both want you to know how much we love you. If you need anything, we can get on the next plane...or buy you a return ticket home.*

Mari knew her mom meant well, but she still felt the heavy weight of the emotion in her mother's texts. Especially Donna's use of the word *father*, as though to remind Mari of who her real dad was. *I promise I'm fine. Please get some sleep, and I'll call you once I'm settled in.*

Without waiting for another response, she turned the ringer off and slid her phone back into her purse.

As she rolled her bags toward the stairs, she knocked over several stacks of books on the floor. At the moment, however, she was too sleep-deprived to care. After much huffing and puffing and a stubbed toe, she finally brought all of her bags up the stairs to the landing outside the door to the flat.

Having faced her first big moment of truth in the store, she didn't make any ceremony of pausing in anticipation before unlocking the flat's door with yet another heavy key.

Yup, no surprises were forthcoming. The flat was as filthy as the store.

Instead of gaping, she simply brought her things inside. The combined kitchen and living room was a decent size, certainly big enough to hold her suitcases until she could find a clean spot to unpack them. She walked down a small hallway that led toward two bedrooms and a bathroom. Every room was a mess.

Clearly, her definition of *perfectly livable* and the solicitor's were very different.

Of course she was thrilled to have an entire bookstore at her disposal. Who wouldn't be? But before she could dive into the treasure trove of books, she'd need to clean the flat so that she would be able to cook and eat and bathe and sleep.

Still, the exhilaration of actually being here, after so long spent dreaming about it, was fluttering inside her. It would take much more than some dust and disorganization to squash her excitement.

First things first. She needed to put some clean sheets on the mattress in the second bedroom. She'd barely poked her head into her father's bedroom—it was too much to deal with all at once—so she certainly couldn't sleep there.

Fifteen minutes later, she had found a stack of crumpled paperwork, old checkbooks, more books, and ceramic bowls in a multitude of shapes and sizes. No sheets or clean towels, however.

Maybe the smart thing to do would be to see if the

pub had a room for the night, so she could return to the store and flat well rested and ready to begin cleanup. But she'd promised herself that she wouldn't falter at the first hurdle—and no matter which way she turned it over inside her head, leaving Charlie's flat within minutes of arriving didn't feel right. It felt like hiding. Like folding under pressure. Like giving in and giving up before she'd even tried to see beyond the dust and disarray.

She would simply have to find a nearby store, buy some clean sheets and towels, take a quick nap, and then get to work.

"Hello? Marina, is that you?"

The sound of the deep male voice—and a positively swoon-worthy British accent—coming from the store downstairs startled her.

Giving her head a shake to try to clear the sleepy cobwebs from her brain, she realized it must be the solicitor coming to greet her, despite her request to remain alone during her first day here. Although she didn't remember his voice having this effect on her when they'd spoken on the phone.

"Coming," she called back.

But before she could get past her suitcases, the best-looking man she'd ever seen appeared in the open doorway.

CHAPTER FOUR

For the first time in his life, Owen Sullivan was rendered completely speechless. Not only by the filthy state of Charlie's bookshop and flat, but also by the woman standing in the middle of it all.

Owen was no stranger to beautiful women. But Marina was different.

She was Charlie's surprise daughter.

And she was, on the surface at least, absolutely *breathtaking*.

Owen's sister Alice had found a few pictures of Marina on the Internet, but none of them did her justice. Standing before him in the grotty flat, she was luminous in jeans, a jumper, and trainers. Her auburn hair tumbled in waves past her shoulders, and there was a flush of color across her high cheekbones and full lips.

He hadn't known what to expect. No one on Elderflower Island had. But he certainly hadn't thought he'd have such a visceral reaction to Charlie's daughter.

Owen had spent so much time in Charlie's flat over the years that it was second nature to let himself in. He didn't want Marina to feel in any way threatened by a presumptuous Englishman, however, so he remained standing in the doorway.

"I'm Owen Sullivan. You must be Charlie's daughter, Marina."

"Mari," she corrected.

"It's nice to finally meet you, Mari."

She winced slightly at his use of the word *finally*. "Are you one of the solicitors?"

"No." He'd initially trained to become a solicitor, but it hadn't been the right fit for him. "Charlie was a good friend. I'm sorry for your loss."

Marina murmured a thank-you. And as they eyed each other in silence across the flat, Owen couldn't help but wonder yet again: Why had Charlie never spoken of Mari?

Charlie had been a fixture on Elderflower Island for nearly thirty years. A gentle, soft-spoken soul, he wouldn't hurt a fly. Which was what made the situation even stranger. Everyone had been shocked to learn that Charlie had a daughter. As far as Owen knew, there hadn't been a will. And the news that Mari had inherited the shop and flat had stunned the small, tight-knit island community.

Owen had always thought the island was too small for anyone to keep a secret.

How wrong he'd been.

He had felt quite close to Charlie, due in large part to his job managing Owen's grandmother's writing career. Not only had Mathilda Westcott been inspired to write her wildly successful *Bookshop on the River* mystery series because of her love for Charlie's shop, but whenever Owen had needed information for one of his grandmother's many international licensing deals, Charlie had never failed to come through for him when Google hadn't been able to turn up an answer.

What's more, over the years, Owen had wondered more than once if his grandmother and Charlie were more than just good friends. Especially given that after Mathilda had begun to recover from her stroke the previous year, the one place she made sure to go every afternoon, no matter how long it took her to walk down the street with her cane, was Charlie's bookshop. She'd sit in her favorite faded green velvet chair and reread the pages she'd written that morning on her work-in-progress, making notes in the margins in purple ink.

Owen's grandmother had been the first to learn of Charlie's illness. And she was the last person Charlie let inside the shop before he had locked it up and kept everyone away.

Owen had wanted to ignore the CLOSED sign on Charlie's door and do whatever he could to help their friend. They all had. But his grandmother, in her soft-spoken but firm way, had insisted they respect Charlie's wishes.

What's more, when news of Mari's existence came to light, Mathilda was the only one who hadn't seemed surprised. His grandmother hadn't been one to gossip while Charlie was alive, and she hadn't divulged any of his secrets since his death either. She had insisted, however, that Owen meet Charlie's daughter upon her arrival from California so that Mari wouldn't feel all alone in a strange new place.

Owen had already planned to go meet Mari, of course. Having spent the past ten years building and protecting his grandmother's legacy, he'd come prepared to defend Charlie's legacy on Elderflower Island, as well.

But instead of a possible adversary waiting inside Charlie's flat, he'd found a beautiful woman. One who looked absolutely shattered from her trip across the pond.

As the oldest of five—and as part of an extended family of Sullivans around the world who always looked out for one another—Owen didn't have it in his DNA not to help someone who needed it. If any of his sisters ended up in a new country where they didn't know a soul, he hoped a stranger would reach out to them.

"I'm sure you must be tired from your flight," he

said, breaking the silence that had stretched out between them. "What can I do to help you settle in? Help you wade through things in Charlie's kitchen so that you can have a cup of tea, perhaps?" It was the British way, after all.

He could all but see her fighting within herself over whether to pretend she had everything under control, when it was abundantly clear that cleaning up the flat was a job for a full cleaning crew, rather than a lone, jet-lagged American.

Finally, she said, "You wouldn't happen to know where Charlie kept the clean sheets, would you?"

Silently noting that she called Charlie by his name, rather than referring to him as *Dad* or *my father*, Owen replied, "I'm afraid not." He scanned the room and decided there was no point in continuing to dance around the obvious. "But even once you find sheets, this place is still a shambles."

"It's not that bad," she said. "I just need to clean it. Then everything will be fine."

Though she did her utmost to sound like she meant it, Owen wasn't convinced. It was on the tip of his tongue to ask her if she would like to stay at his place for a night or two. But he didn't want her to think that he'd been lying in wait for her to arrive so that he could take advantage of her.

Instead, he said, "I'm sure my mother, or one of

my sisters, would be more than happy to put you up until the flat is more livable."

She looked surprised by his offer. "They don't even know me. I could be a total whack job, for all you know."

"You're Charlie's daughter. They need no other reason." He smiled as he added, "And, at first glance at least, you don't seem to fit the profile of a *whack job*."

"I'm sorry," she said suddenly. "You've been nothing but nice—and I've been nothing but rude." She finally gave him a small smile of her own, one that lit up her face. "Could we start over? Hi, I'm Mari Everett. Come on in."

For the second time in five minutes, Owen found himself speechless.

His father, Simon, liked to tell the story of the first time he'd set eyes on their mother, Penny, claiming that he'd known immediately he was going to marry her. Though Owen had always been comforted by the fact that his parents were a true-love match, at the same time, he had never understood how such a huge rush of feeling could completely override all rational thought.

He didn't know anything about Mari beyond the fact that she was Charlie's daughter, but Owen was shaken to realize that one small smile was enough to make him understand what had happened to his father.

Owen had never felt less rational in his life as his heart whispered, *She's the one.*

Giving his head a shake, he reminded himself that taking care of his grandmother while she continued to heal from her stroke and running Mathilda's literary business came first. Everything else would have to take a backseat.

Including the mad sensation of having been struck by Cupid's arrow.

Belatedly realizing Mari was still waiting for him to respond to both her apology and her invitation, he stepped inside the flat for their do-over. "Hello, I'm Owen Sullivan, Charlie's friend."

He reached out to shake her hand, struck by the warmth moving through him from her hand in his. He could see dark smudges of exhaustion beneath her eyes...and was pretty sure her stomach had just rumbled. "Have you had anything to eat or drink since you've arrived?"

She shook her head. Reluctantly, he let her hand go as she turned to look at the kitchen. Dirty mugs and plates covered the counter and filled the sink. "You're right that the flat is a mess. I'm not sure I'm going to find anything in the kitchen that won't kill me." A beat after *kill me* landed, she winced.

More and more certain that she wasn't a villainess out to pilfer her father's legacy for riches, Owen said,

"Why don't you let me sort out some sheets and food for you? My office is on the other side of the boatyard. It won't take me long to head there and back."

"I hate to impose..." She gave him another small smile. "But I can't tell you how grateful clean sheets and something to eat would make me. That is, if you're not too busy. Because I can find stores in town that sell sheets and food."

Though Owen's afternoon workload was tightly packed, he'd never forgive himself if Mari keeled over in the middle of the House of Fraser department store or the M&S Food Hall. "It's no problem," he insisted. "I'll only be a short while."

He took the stairs down two at a time and let himself out of the store. Turning left, he headed past the boathouse toward the row of picturesque, pastel-painted cottages that starred on the cover of more than one travel guide to England. At the end of the lane sat his grandmother's house and garden.

Nearly every day for the past twenty-five years, Mathilda Westcott had sat at the old wooden table by the window with a cup of tea and a notebook and pen to write her books. As the popularity of her *Bookshop on the River* series had steadily grown over the years, so had her need for someone she trusted implicitly to manage her business affairs. Ten years earlier, when Owen was twenty-six and working in tax law, his grandmother had asked him to oversee her contracts, coordinate her conference and fan events around the globe, and negotiate her licensing deals across TV, film, stage, audio, and foreign translations.

Mathilda hadn't traveled out of the area since her stroke, and Owen knew she missed the interaction with her readers as much as her fans missed getting the opportunity to meet her. After all these years, her fans had become something much closer to family.

Owen owed his grandmother more than he could ever repay. She'd not only given him the chance for a new career when she'd recognized that tax law wasn't his passion—she also had no idea just how badly he'd let her down last year.

Yet again, he wished he could rewind time and be there for her that morning she'd started to slightly slur her words. If only he had been able to spot the signs of a stroke and call an ambulance immediately, rather than hours later, when he'd finally returned to the office where he should have been all along, rather than at a clandestine meeting he never should have agreed to.

Unfortunately, he couldn't turn back time. All he could do was keep watch over his grandmother to make sure he didn't miss the signs of a second stroke—and work twice as hard to grow her business, though he knew that would never come close to making amends.

Owen's home was a mile away on Richmond Hill, but since his grandmother's stroke, he'd moved into her garden cottage, which was equipped with a bed, a small kitchenette, and a full bath. Though Mathilda repeatedly encouraged him to go out, he couldn't stand the thought that something might happen again while he was gone, which meant he'd barely seen his friends this past year, let alone dated.

His grandmother put down her pen when he walked in. "I didn't expect you back so soon." She'd made great strides in her recovery, but if you listened closely, her diction was slightly slower than it had been before her stroke. After a particularly long day, her words would sometimes slur a bit. Fortunately, today they sounded crisp and distinct. "Did you speak with Marina? What is she like?"

"She's very nice. And she prefers to be called Mari." He knew how curious his grandmother was about Charlie's daughter. Before last year, Owen had no doubt that Mathilda would have been the one to greet Mari upon her arrival. But social interactions—especially with new people—still tired her out. "The flat is a mess, so I offered to find her some clean sheets and something to eat, as well. I imagine she isn't thrilled about the cleanup awaiting her. I had no idea the shop or the flat were in that bad of a state."

"I was afraid Charlie would let it all go." His grandmother sighed, looking upset. She was still grieving for Charlie. They all were. "What else can you tell me about Mari?"

"We didn't speak for very long, but I get the sense that Charlie's death and her inheritance have both come as a huge shock."

"I'm sure they have," his grandmother said in a soft voice.

"Gran, what do you know about Mari? What did Charlie tell you about their relationship—or absence thereof?"

She shook her head. "You know I would never divulge something shared in confidence. What I will say, however, is that I'm very happy to know you're here to help her through the rough patches."

"Of course I want to help her. But I can't abandon you and your business affairs."

"You are the most wonderful grandson I could wish for. With that said, you've spent *far* too long babysitting me since my stroke. I'm feeling just fine, and I insist that you give Mari as much of your time and help as she needs, both today and in the weeks to come."

Owen was extremely glad to hear his grandmother felt so well. The first four months of her recovery had been intense as she worked to regain both her speech and the use of the right side of her body. Thankfully, during the past eight months, she'd gone from strength to strength. Still, he couldn't simply shake off his worries. In addition to making sure she ate properly, got regular exercise, and took her medications, he was constantly checking for signs of another stroke.

She reached for his hand. "I promise you, darling, I feel right as rain. Mari is the one who needs you now."

He pressed a kiss to her cheek, her signature elderflower scent enveloping him. "Text or call if you need anything. My mobile will be on, as always."

He was just turning to collect food and sheets, when his grandmother called him back. "I forgot to ask—is she as lovely as the pictures we found on the Internet?"

Owen pictured Mari's flushed cheeks, full lips, and flowing hair. "Even lovelier."

CHAPTER FIVE

Owen headed back to the bookshop with two bags—one containing a set of sheets and a duvet cover, the other stuffed full of teabags, scones, clotted cream, jam, and the flowers Alice had brought by Mathilda's cottage earlier that morning.

His personal assistant, Gael, who worked remotely from Edinburgh, was rescheduling his afternoon meetings. One with a director and writer from a French TV production company that wanted to create a twelve-episode series from his grandmother's books. Another with a digital media company interested in converting his grandmother's books into a graphically rich reading experience.

Gael had clearly been shocked to hear that he was taking some impromptu time off today, particularly after he'd reassured her that Mathilda's health wasn't the reason for his bunking off so suddenly. He would make up the hours tonight, but his grandmother was absolutely right that he couldn't simply deliver sheets and food to Mari, then leave her to deal with the mess in the flat by herself.

As Mari was expecting him this time, he let himself into the bookshop before calling out, "I'm back with supplies." Though there was no reply, he started up the stairs. The door to the flat was still ajar, but when he knocked, she still didn't respond.

"Mari?" He poked his head in the doorway…and found her fast asleep on the leather sofa in the living room.

She had cleaned off enough space to curl herself up into a ball, her head resting on her open palm rather than on one of the dusty pillows. She was still wearing her trainers, which made him think she hadn't planned to fall asleep. Before his grandmother's stroke, Owen had traveled extensively for work—and play. He knew firsthand how hard jet lag could hit you.

Even in sleep, Mari's brow was slightly furrowed. Still, her beauty shone through, pure and lovely.

So lovely, in fact, that she stole his breath away all over again.

Not wanting to trespass in her private space, he considered leaving the bags at the door. But he couldn't shake his concern over the state of the flat. Nor could he simply walk out without helping in some concrete way.

Given that he had already canceled his meetings and now had the afternoon free, it seemed a waste not to get started cleaning the flat while she was sleeping. Hopefully, she wouldn't freak out when she woke to find him there.

Walking quietly into the open-plan kitchen, he put the bag of food down amongst the clutter, then headed down the hall. In Charlie's bedroom to the right, his friend's jacket was still hanging on the valet beside the door, his shoes beneath it.

Owen's chest clenched. Charlie's death had been a major blow to the entire island community. Not only had he kept his illness a secret for months, blaming his weight loss and pallor on a lingering flu—but once his cancer diagnosis had come out, he had refused to seek treatment. In his final weeks, he had isolated himself from everyone, closing the bookshop and locking the door. The ambulance sirens had sounded the dreaded death knell.

And Elderflower Island hadn't been the same since.

Closing Charlie's bedroom door, Owen went into the second bedroom, guessing that was where Mari would prefer to sleep. Though the guest room was less cluttered than Charlie's room, it was still in desperate need of a hoovering. Since that would wake Mari, he would have to be content with airing and dusting the room and putting fresh sheets on the bed. He wanted to do something that would help her feel a little more comfortable in her new home. One that Owen, along with everyone else, wondered if she intended to keep.

If she had come with the expectation of finding the bookshop as it had been in its heyday, she must be sorely disappointed. What, he wondered again, had kept her from coming until after her father's death? Had they been in touch all these years? Had she deliberately stayed away? Or had Charlie insisted their relationship remain a secret for some reason? Hopefully, she would be willing to provide some answers.

Owen opened the French doors that led to the Juliet balcony off the guest bedroom and wiped down the room's hard surfaces with a cleaning rag. Next, he stripped the mattress, pillow, and duvet and remade the bed with fresh linen, putting the dusty sheets into his bag to take home to wash.

Upon returning to the living room and finding that Mari hadn't stirred from her spot on the couch, he decided to tackle the kitchen. Growing up in a crowded, busy house, he'd been taught how to cook and clean. As kids, they'd each had a room that was their responsibility. Owen's had been the kitchen.

Thankfully, there were several mostly full bottles of cleaning supplies in the cupboard beneath the sink. For all of Charlie's many positive aspects and good intentions, he hadn't been much for keeping things tidy. His part-time staff had taken care of cleaning the bookshop, and a cleaner would come to the flat once every month or so with a mop and duster. Still, the rooms had never reached anywhere near this state before.

Working as quietly as possible, Owen washed and dried the dirty mugs, dishes, and silverware littering the kitchen surfaces. He dusted the windowsills, cleaned the windows that overlooked the river until they sparkled, and polished the sink fixtures. The small refrigerator was in a horrifying state, particularly from an olfactory perspective. Owen held his breath as he got on with clearing out the rotting rinds of cheese, the molding pasta sauce, and the bunch of grapes that had liquefied, so he could wipe down the shelves and drawers. At last, he laid the blue-painted kitchen table with scones, clotted cream, and jam, along with a teacup and saucer.

"Owen?"

He turned to find Mari sitting up on the couch, her hair tangled on one side, her left cheek lightly imprinted with the outline of the small gold ring on her pinky finger.

"Feeling better now that you've had some rest?"

She nodded as she ran a hand through her hair. "The last thing I remember is sitting down." Her words were slightly husky now, and though her jeans and jumper were rumpled, she still wore them with natural grace. "How long have you been back?"

"A couple of hours." He beckoned her into the kitchen as he put the kettle on for tea. "Why don't you have something to eat and drink?"

Her eyes were huge as she looked around the kitchen. "You did this while I was sleeping?" She gaped at the clear countertops, at the pristine stove top, at the vase of bright flowers, and at the smudge-free windows. "Not only bringing me food and flowers, but cleaning the *entire* room?" He thought she just might throw herself into his arms out of sheer gratitude. "How can I ever repay you?"

"As I said before, I'm happy to help." He smiled as he added, "No repayment is necessary."

"Thank you." She looked a little shy as she asked, "Will you at least join me in eating the food you brought?"

"I'd like that." He set another place at the table. "Does builder's tea sound all right?"

"That's really strong black tea, isn't it?"

"Strong enough to strip the paint off these walls." Which, frankly, looked like they *did* need to be stripped and repainted.

"Sounds perfect."

He was gratified to see her lavish clotted cream and his sister's homemade strawberry jam on a scone, then hungrily dig in.

"This is so good." Her sentence, spoken around a

mouthful, came out as one long string of sound.

"My sister Alice will be glad to hear you think so. I know she's looking forward to meeting you. Everyone is."

Mari put down the scone, looking a little wary again. "It sounds like all of you knew my father really well."

"We did." At least they'd thought so. "Although none of us knew about you."

"He left when I was three." A shadow crossed her face. "I never heard from him again."

Owen's heart broke for her. What possible reason could Charlie have had to leave his own daughter? And then never speak to anyone of her again...

"I'm sorry, Mari."

"I'm sorry too." Clearly uncomfortable with their line of conversation, she stood up and began clearing away the food. "You've been so helpful, and I'm really grateful, but I don't want to take up any more of your day. I should let you go."

Knowing he should heed her request to be alone, even if he thought it was the last thing she needed right now, as he also stood, he felt compelled to say, "Any questions you want to ask about Charlie, about his life or business, I'm happy to answer as best I can. I know you've just gotten off a plane, and I'm sure you want to spend some time getting settled in, but perhaps tomorrow I could take you to breakfast and do my best to fill in some gaps?"

She stared at him, clearly bemused. "You're being so nice to me. Did he mean that much to you?"

"He did. And trust me when I say that I completely understand how, when it comes to family, things aren't always as straightforward as we would like them to be."

"Family." The word was barely more than a whisper of sound from her lips. "I don't know if only knowing him for three years counts."

"Maybe," he said softly, "I can help you figure out the answer to that by answering some of your questions."

She was silent as she pondered the possibility. Finally, she nodded. "Breakfast tomorrow sounds good."

★ ★ ★

A text from Alice buzzed onto Owen's mobile as he was leaving, the bag of dirty sheets to wash back at the cottage slung over his shoulder.

Malc and I bunked off early to get a drink at the pub. Meet us there?

For the past year, Owen had turned down offers from both family and friends to meet up so that he could stay close to his grandmother at all hours. Today, however, Mathilda had been fiercer than usual in her insistence that he get out more. His parents and siblings had also mentioned more than once that they were concerned about his becoming a hermit. Still, his gut clenched at the thought that something might happen to his grandmother while he was gone, especially since it had been hours since he'd last seen her.

He was just typing in a message telling Alice that he'd take a rain check, when a follow-up text came through from his sister.

I'm with Gran now. She says she feels great, and she's planning to binge-watch a new cooking show. She insists you "live a little" and come to the pub with us.

Just as he'd said to Mari, family wasn't always straightforward. But that didn't mean love wasn't there. He didn't intend to smother his grandmother—all he wanted was to make things right. Clearly, today that meant giving her some space.

Only twenty yards from the pub, he texted Alice to let her know he'd grab a table and the first round.

Ten minutes later, his sister burst through the doors. Her jeans were covered in their usual layer of potting soil, her cheeks were rosy from working outdoors, and she was wearing a faded cap with *Kew Gardens* stitched on the front.

"It's a miracle! You're actually here for a drink." Alice pinched herself, then him. "Just making sure neither of us is dreaming." Barely pausing for breath, she said, "Gran said you met Charlie's daughter. I looked in the bookshop window, but I didn't see any signs of life. Tell me *everything*."

Malcolm strode in just then, looking every inch the businessman in his bespoke Italian suit and polished leather shoes. Fortunately, on the inside he was still the same rugby-playing, down-to-earth guy he'd been when they were kids.

"Perfect timing, Malc." Alice kissed him hello on both cheeks. "Owen is just about to give us the dirt on Charlie's daughter."

Owen tensed at the word *dirt*. Now that he'd met Mari, he regretted the way everyone on the island, including him, had been prepared to assume the worst about her.

"First of all, Mari loved your scones and jam."

"Mari?" Alice asked. "I thought her name was Marina."

"She prefers Mari. In any case, she was exhausted and hungry after her flight. It didn't help that the shop and flat are a complete mess. After saying hello and seeing the state of the place, I went back to Gran's for clean sheets and food, helped clean up the flat a bit, and made her tea."

Alice put down her drink and looked more closely at him. "You like her."

"She could barely keep her eyes open and napped

for a while, so we didn't spend that much time talking. But yes, I like her." More than he'd liked anyone in a very long time.

Malcolm didn't look convinced. "What's her story?"

Of the five of them, Malc was the most analytical. He demanded facts, rather than guesses or estimations. It was one of the reasons his multimillion-pound business deals rarely, if ever, went wrong.

"I don't know much yet," Owen replied, "and even if I did, Mari's story would be best coming directly from her. But what I can tell you is that it isn't her fault we didn't know about her until now." Any way he turned things over inside his head, he couldn't understand how Charlie could have left Mari when she was only a toddler. Never talked to her again. Never held her again.

Alice took a sip of her lime and soda, considering. "I still can't believe he kept her from all of us."

"Sometimes," Malcolm said, "even when you want to be with someone, that doesn't mean it's possible." This wasn't the first time over the years that he had made a cryptic statement along those lines. But just as he had every time before, he pivoted. "When are you seeing her again?"

"Tomorrow for breakfast."

Alice whistled. "Not only did you do the unthinkable and take time off work this afternoon to help clean her flat, but you're taking off even more time to see her tomorrow morning! She's obviously made a huge impression on you—we haven't seen you emerge from the office this much in a full year. Now I'm *really* dying to meet her."

"I honestly can't imagine Mari had any idea of what she was walking into," Owen told them. "She's going to need a lot of help cleaning the place up and getting the shop back into some kind of working order again."

"Did she tell you whether she's planning to keep it?" Malcolm asked.

"As I said, we didn't get that far." And even if they had, it didn't feel right to sit with his brother and sister and speculate about her intentions. "Tell me, what's blooming in the garden—and in the world of highflying business deals?"

It was a clear cue to move on from discussing Charlie's daughter. A cue his sister surely wouldn't want to heed, but thankfully she did as she told them about her day aerating compost heaps at Kew Gardens. No wonder she smelled particularly earthy today—she'd been all but rolling in organic soil since eight that morning.

She nudged Malcolm. "My workday is pretty different from your day in your climate-controlled skyscraper, isn't it, Mr. Highflier?"

"Not as different as you'd think." He grimaced. "Negotiating my newest deal felt exactly like diving into a compost heap."

When Alice laughed, Owen realized he'd checked out of the conversation. "Sorry, what was that?"

"Never mind." His sister grinned. "Keep daydreaming about the American bookshop heiress, while I get the next round."

CHAPTER SIX

Mari cleaned the flat all afternoon and long into the night, jet lag keeping her awake while the rest of London was sleeping. It wasn't until she had finished mopping the kitchen floor that she finally stopped to take it in.

This was my father's home.

It still didn't seem quite real, that she was actually here, surrounded by his furniture, his pictures, his cups and plates, his art on the walls. Once she'd woken from her nap—and with the mess cleared away—Mari could see just how charming the flat was.

Her mother's home and Charlie's flat were as different as night and day. Where the Spanish-style California rancher was decorated with brightly colored ceramic tiles on the floor and countertops, had every modern convenience in the kitchen and bathrooms, and featured a large green lawn out in the backyard, the London flat had old floorboards, a clawfoot tub in the bathroom, and a stunning view over the river. Every time Mari looked out the window, as day turned to night, the river was different. Calm, then rising, then fast-flowing, and now, as the moon rose high in the sky, calm again.

How, she wondered, would her mother react if Mari did a video walk-through next time they spoke? Not well, that was for sure.

Oh no, how could she have forgotten? Mari had promised to check in with her parents tonight before bed, but she had neither gone to sleep, nor remembered to charge her phone. Rummaging through her bags for a power converter, she plugged in her cell. As soon as it came to life, a half-dozen missed calls—and many more texts—buzzed through. All were different versions of the same panicky message from her mother, apart from one from Carson.

Hope you're having a great time. Tried to talk Mom off the ledge when she didn't hear from you tonight, but you can guess how well that went. Text anytime if you need to chat.

Calling her parents from Charlie's flat didn't feel right, so once her phone's battery had been sufficiently charged, Mari headed downstairs and out through the store that seemed in even worse disarray at second glance. The street outside was quiet and empty, the sky clear, and the moon shimmered over a river as smooth as glass.

It was one of the prettiest scenes imaginable.

Wishing she'd had more than that short nap on the

couch to restore her fried brain cells before this call, she dialed her parents' house.

"Mari?" Her mother picked up on the first ring. "Thank God. We thought something had happened to you."

"I'm fine, I just got busy and then my phone battery died."

"What have you been busy with?" Her mother was instantly suspicious. "The flat and store are both dumps, aren't they? Just like I said they would be."

Mari didn't believe in lying to her parents, which was why she was glad she could say honestly, "The flat is quite nice, actually."

"What about the bookstore?"

"That's going to take some reorganization." Also true. "But I'm sure once I dig in, I'll be able to sort it out quickly." She dearly hoped that last part ended up being true.

"The quicker the better," her mother said.

Mari's gut clenched as she thought of going back to Santa Monica. Though she'd been in London only half a day and had been holed up inside the flat for nearly all of it, she'd found everything she'd seen and experienced so far—the buildings and the river and the delicious scone and jam and wallpaper-stripping tea—to be wonderful.

Especially her unexpected savior, Owen Sullivan.

Before she'd set eyes on him, just the sound of his super-sexy British accent had set her insides ablaze. And once she'd actually seen him...

Frankly, she'd never thought lust at first sight was something that would ever happen to her. Then again, she'd never counted on meeting Owen.

At first, he'd seemed slightly suspicious of her, as though he assumed she'd come to London to sell off her father's things to the lowest bidder. It hadn't stopped him from being extremely kind, however. He'd not only brought her food—he'd cleaned her kitchen too!

Her mother's next question broke through her thoughts. "Has anyone poked their nose into your business? Tried to get the dirt on you?"

"One of Charlie's friends came by to see if I needed anything."

"I can only imagine what kind of *friend* it was. Probably one he met at the bottom of a bottle of whiskey."

"Actually," Mari said in Owen's defense, "he was very nice and wanted to know if he could bring me something to eat after my long trip."

"Hmmm." If anything, her mother sounded more mistrustful now. "Maybe he's planning to play a longer game with you. Reel you in until he lulls you with his charming accent into a false sense of security and then—"

"Mom!" Mari understood that her mother was worried about her—especially about her life unraveling if she fell for an unsuitable Brit—but after all the help Owen had given her this afternoon, she couldn't let Donna continue down that road. "Owen isn't playing any kind of game with me."

"I certainly hope not. I didn't raise you to be anyone's fool. Or to fall for a good-looking man with an accent the way I did."

Mari's cheeks flushed in the cool night air as she silently acknowledged just how good-looking Owen was. And her mother wasn't wrong that his British accent made her insides feel...*melty*.

"I know you want to honor your birth father," Donna said in a gentler voice. "Not many people would put their lives on hold out of respect for someone who, frankly, didn't deserve it. Though I'm not pleased with any of this, I'm also not surprised by how charitable you're being, given that Gary and I have raised you to be a kind person. Charlie is far luckier than he ever knew."

Amazingly, from everything Owen had said about Charlie that afternoon, it seemed Mari's father truly *had* been lucky with his bookstore and a bevy of friends on the island. Which only made Mari's gut churn more.

Because if his life had come to be so great once he left California and moved to Elderflower Island, why hadn't he reached out to her at that point? Had he been afraid that seeing or speaking to her would somehow mess things up for him again?

"He never tried to contact me through you when I was growing up, did he?" She had been only five years old when she'd realized the one thing guaranteed to send her mother reeling into tears and darkness was to ask questions about Charlie. So Mari had stopped asking. Now that she was on his home turf, however, it was impossible to continue to keep her questions inside.

"Of course he didn't!"

A heavy silence hung between them. Jet lag clearly did no favors for either Mari's self-control or her timing, considering a question like that was guaranteed to set her mother off. "I'm glad I was able to reach you, but I should try to get some sleep."

"Okay, sleep well. And be sure to call me tomorrow to let me know how things are progressing—and what day to expect you back."

"Actually..." Mari was compelled to say one more thing before they disconnected. "I think it might be best if I spare you the day-to-day details. I'd like to take a little time to try to sort things out a bit more and wrap my head around my inheritance."

"What are you saying?" Her mother's voice vibrated with concern. "That you don't want to talk with me or your father while you're in Charlie's world?"

"No, that's not it at all." Mari tried to explain in a way her mother might understand. "Just like with any business, it's going to take some time for me to assess the bookstore's viability. I lost track of time today, and since I suspect I will again, I hate to think of either of you waiting up for my phone calls. I promise I'll be in touch with any big news, but I don't want you to worry if you don't hear from me for a few days."

Her mother didn't reply for long enough that Mari knew Donna was either about to blow up at her or start crying. Of course she didn't want to upset her mom, but at the same time, she did, in fact, need some space to work through all of the changes in her life. Though she loved her parents dearly, she'd known better than to let them dictate her choices six weeks ago when she'd decided to come to Elderflower Island, and she couldn't make that mistake now either.

"Well," her mother finally said, "in that case, we won't hold our breath waiting for your next call."

"Mom." Her voice was gentle. "You know the last thing I want to do is upset you or Dad."

She heard her mother's shaky exhalation over the phone line. "I know. And I trust you to do the right thing, honey. Of course I do. It's just that I also know how enticing exotic things can be. Enticing enough for me to lose my head when I was your age. But you've always been strong and smart, so I'll do my best to heed your wishes and stop worrying about you."

"Thanks, Mom. I love you."

"Love you too, honey. Good night."

After hanging up, Mari didn't immediately head back inside. The evening was too beautiful, with the rising moon sparkling on the river and the air smelling sweeter and fresher than it ever did in Santa Monica. A black cat sashayed past, eyeing her up before slinking over to the front door of the bookstore and sitting in front of it.

Mari had always wanted a cat, but her stepfather was allergic to dander. "Are you another one of Charlie's friends?"

The cat didn't answer, of course. It simply lifted one paw to give it a leisurely lick. When she opened the door, it sauntered inside as if it owned the place, then hopped up onto the counter by the register, curled into a ball, and closed its eyes.

Perhaps it was foolish to leave a cat she didn't know inside the store, but honestly, the animal couldn't make things any messier. "Good night," Mari told it, then went upstairs to finally get some sleep of her own.

CHAPTER SEVEN

Morning dawned bright through the guest bedroom window. Mari had intended to take a bath before falling asleep, but by the time she'd walked upstairs, it had been all she could do to strip off her clothes and slide beneath the clean sheets Owen had put on the double bed.

So many things were different in England. The architecture, the accents, the history—even drawing herself a bath rather than taking a quick shower. Slipping into the hot water and lying in the clawfoot tub felt indulgent. And extremely necessary, given how much her muscles ached from her hours of cleaning the previous night.

As she soaped up her skin with an orange-scented bar, she couldn't help but think about Owen. Though she barely knew him, her heart raced as she wondered what it would be like if he did this for her instead.

When her stomach rumbled, she realized with a jolt back to reality just how crazy her thoughts were, considering they had only just met the day before.

Last night, by the time she'd polished off the rest of the scones, clotted cream, and jam, the corner market had been closed, and it had been too late to venture out to find an open grocery off the island. Charlie's cupboards were bare apart from a can of baked beans and something called *spotted dick*. Upon reading the ingredient list, she learned that it was a suet and dried fruit dessert. Another day, she'd try it. Thankfully, this morning she had breakfast plans with a very handsome local.

Fifteen minutes later, she was dressed and ready to go. Owen wouldn't arrive for a half hour or so, which gave her enough time to venture back into the bookstore in the light of day.

Even dusty, dirty piles of books were wonderful, of course. But this wasn't just *any* bookstore. Her father had chosen each of the books on the shelves, the armchairs for people to sit in to read, the rugs on the floor, the framed prints on the walls. What's more, in order to make a decision about what to do with the bookstore—whether to sell it or to keep it and run it herself—she needed to find out what state the business was in. Which meant finding the account books, as well as the local business regulation handbooks and customer lists.

After heading down the stairs from the flat to the store, she slowly scanned the space and was surprised to realize there was a garden patio out back. Had Charlie's customers enjoyed taking a book out into the sunshine with a cup of tea? And given the completely overgrown state of it, how long would it take her to turn the small garden into a place where someone would actually want to sit in the future?

A *meow* from the counter by the register startled her. She had forgotten about the little black cat. In truth, much of yesterday had a blurry feel to it.

The cat stood and stretched, then hopped off the counter and made for the front door. Mari picked her way through the pile of books on the floor to let it out. She watched as it raced across the street and headed for the Fox & Hound. Obviously, it knew exactly where to go to find food.

She had long dreamed of eating at a British pub. But how would the owner, and the other locals, react once they knew she was Charlie's daughter? Would they assume she had abandoned her father and hate her for it, given that Charlie was clearly a local hero? Then again, Owen's suspicions had instantly dropped away once she'd blurted out the truth about Charlie's leaving.

At a glance, there seemed to be no rhyme or reason to the bookstore. She hoped it was just a bad first impression. Reminding herself that she always enjoyed creating order from chaos while at the office, she forced herself to approach the situation as though she was working with a client who had inherited the store. First, she would need to pull together anything related to sales and inventory.

Figuring those files might be located near the register, she made her way through the piles of books. Halfway across the room, a copy of *Winnie-the-Pooh* caught her eye.

One of her crystal-clear memories of her father, apart from playing conkers together, was how Charlie would read the book to her before bed nearly every night, doing different voices for each character. After he had gone, the popular children's book had felt like her only remaining link to him.

At twenty-two, she'd taken her first paycheck from the accounting firm and bought fourth-edition copies of *Winnie-the-Pooh* and *The House at Pooh Corner*. Over the years, she'd added to her collection whenever she could.

Picking up the book, she dusted it off with her fingertips, then opened the cover. She could hardly believe her eyes. Not only was it a first edition from 1926, but it was also signed by both A.A. Milne, the author, and E.H. Shepard, the illustrator.

Her hands shook as she held the book to her chest. It wasn't just that she knew the book was worth an absolute fortune. What moved her far more was that finding it felt like an omen. A good one. As though her father had left the book here in the hopes that she'd see it and think of their time together...

A knock at the door jolted her out of her musings. Still clutching the book to her chest, she went to let Owen in.

Though the air outside was chilly, his smile warmed her. "Good morning. I know I'm a little early. I hope that's okay with you."

"It's great." He was even better looking today, if that was possible. "Let me put this book away, and then I'll be ready to go."

Owen cocked his head to read the spine. "Charlie had a particular fondness for Winnie-the-Pooh stories. They're brilliantly written and illustrated, of course, but his interest seemed to go beyond that."

Thinking of her long-ago connection with her father had warmth blooming in Mari's chest as she put the book behind the counter. As she'd hoped, several account registers were stacked on the lower shelves, along with thick book sales catalogs.

"If you don't mind a bit of a walk," Owen said, "I'd like to take you off the island to one of my favorite cafés in Richmond."

"A walk sounds great." She locked up behind them, and then they headed out past the pub and boutiques to the bridge.

The landscape seemed impossibly green, especially to someone who had grown up surrounded by golden hills and droughts that could last for years. What's more, they were barely into their walk when Owen pointed out two blue plaques—markers bestowed upon buildings of historical significance by the English Heritage society. One was for a music studio where the biggest British rock bands of the sixties and seventies had recorded, and the other was for a respected landscape painter from the early 1900s.

A few minutes later, Mari had a perfect view of the Richmond Bridge, the oldest bridge in London. She nearly pinched herself to make sure she wasn't dreaming. "I feel like I'm in a British fairy tale," she said, sounding like a full-fledged tourist.

"Plenty of Brits feel the same way about the US."

She turned to him in surprise. "Really?"

"Most of us grew up on a steady diet of American TV shows and movies." He leaned in and lowered his voice as though he were sharing clandestine information. "We secretly dream of attending an American high school or a baseball game."

Who would have guessed? Smiling, she leaned toward him and said, "My advice? Skip high school and go straight to the game."

He grinned. "Duly noted."

Mari was thankful that Owen had been the first

person to come calling at the bookstore. Though they didn't know each other very well yet, he made her feel like she wasn't in this entirely alone.

"Have you ever lived in the US?" she asked.

"No, but my brother Malcolm did a foreign exchange when he was in sixth form." At her confused look, he clarified, "Sixth form is our last couple of years of high school, when we're studying for our A levels, just before we go to uni. Anyway, he loved it. Enough that if he hadn't been accepted to Cambridge, I'm not sure we'd have gotten him back to the UK."

"How many siblings do you have?"

"There are five of us. I'm the oldest, then Malc, Tom, Fiona, and Alice. And Tom has a five-year-old daughter named Aria. She's adorable." He said each sibling's name and his niece's so fondly that she knew they must be a close-knit family. "What about you?"

"I have one brother, Carson. He's my stepbrother, actually, but my mom married his father when I was four, so it feels like we were always brother and sister."

"How does your family feel about you being here?"

"Carson offered to come with me even though it would have meant completely reorganizing his work schedule. I couldn't let him do that." She paused, unsure of how much more to say. The last thing she wanted was to be disloyal to her mother and stepfather. At the same time, she longed to discuss things with someone who might know more of Charlie's side of the story.

Before she could figure out what to tell Owen about Donna and Gary, he said, "We're here."

She must have been completely lost in her thoughts. Otherwise, she wouldn't have missed entering this beautiful park on a hill, at the center of which sat one of the cutest cafés she'd ever seen. The pillars for the outdoor terrace roof were made from thick tree branches, and the roof was thatched. Several people were having coffee and enjoying the view through the park to the Thames, and young moms were watching their children play together on the grass.

"What a beautiful setting," she marveled.

"The Hollyhock Café is a well-kept local secret. When people come to see the usual round of nearby tourist sites—Kew Gardens, Richmond Park, Turner's View, Pete Townshend's house—this park and café are easy to overlook."

"Thank you for sharing it with me."

He smiled. "You're a local now."

Longing welled up inside her chest. Could she actually pick up here where her father had left off and be an Elderflower Island local?

Or would it be far more sensible to do what her mother had suggested and completely wash her hands of it all? To continue with life in Santa Monica as she'd always known it?

They headed into the café and ordered, then took their hot drinks outside and found a table set slightly apart from those of the other customers. Though Mari knew it would be easier to keep asking questions about Owen's family, or to have him tell her more about Elderflower Island and the surrounding towns, she refused to bury her head in the sand.

"Whatever you know about Charlie," she said, "I'd appreciate hearing it."

"He was a quiet man, and a good one. Possibly more comfortable with his books than with people. But if you ever needed anything, he was there to help. And his bookshop was as much a hub of the island community as the pub."

It was a lot to take in, even though Owen had already given her hints as to just how beloved her father had been. "Did he host a lot of events at his store?"

"Not formally." Owen gave her a rueful grin. "Charlie, as you might already have noticed, wasn't great at organization. But reader groups, and nonbook groups too, still liked to congregate informally in the shop."

"It sounds like it was a really great store while he was alive. Even my taxi driver yesterday told me it was his favorite bookstore in London." Grief hit her again, a stabbing pain to the solar plexus. "I tried to find out about it over the years," she admitted, "but Charlie didn't have a website, so it was hard to glean much information. It sounds like you spent quite a bit of time there."

"I did. And so did my grandmother. She and Charlie were quite close." When Mari's eyebrows went up, Owen clarified, "As far as I know, they were just friends, but she loved his bookshop so much it inspired her mystery series."

"Your grandmother is a writer?"

She could see from his smile how proud he was of his grandmother—and how much he adored her. "She writes the *Bookshop on the River* mystery series."

Mari was floored. "Your grandmother is *Mathilda Westcott?*" When Owen nodded, she said, "I can't believe I didn't know Charlie's store was the inspiration for her series. I've read all of her books multiple times."

"It was one of the few things they argued about," Owen told her. "She wanted to put his name—and the shop—in the acknowledgments of her books, but he refused to let her, even though it would surely have brought him more business. He did relent about allowing the TV series to be filmed in the shop, however."

Mari worked to shake herself out of her mixed

emotions over everything she was learning about her father. "You've made a TV series out of your grandmother's books? And filmed it in the store?"

"Not yet," he clarified. "Actually, it's something I was hoping to speak with you about at some point. I manage Mathilda's career, and we were in the final stages of negotiating with the network when Charlie got sick." He paused, looking apologetic. "I'm sorry. You've asked about your father, and here I am telling you about plans for a TV program."

"It's important, though, isn't it?" Though she felt swamped by emotion from everything she was learning, Mari had to be pragmatic. "Filming a TV show in the store might go a long way toward the feasibility of keeping it open. Depending on what I find in his account books, that is. I'm not sure what you already know about me, but I'm an accountant."

He looked contrite. "I did already know that about you."

"Don't feel bad. I realized last night that you—and everyone else who was close to Charlie—would have wondered who the mystery daughter was and worried enough about my plans for the store to look me up online."

"I'm not going to lie to you, Mari. We were all curious—and worried. But as you said, it's not easy to find out much about someone unless they're active on social media. I didn't know what to expect yesterday."

"And?" Though she didn't blame him for being curious, she couldn't quite keep the challenge from her voice. "How did first impressions measure up?"

"You're very beautiful."

She flushed, his comment taking a great deal of the wind out of her sails. She could feel the heat on her cheeks as she asked, "What does that have to do with anything?"

"You asked me for my impressions, and the truth is that the first thing that struck me is how lovely you are. The second is that you don't seem the least bit mercenary."

Okay, then, he certainly got points for honesty, after making it clear that he both found her attractive and had been half expecting her to be a gold digger.

"I had no idea Charlie would leave me his bookstore and home." Her chest tightened. "I had no idea he thought of me at all, actually."

"Mari." Owen put his hand over hers. "I know we haven't spent much time together yet, but something tells me you're going to do the right thing by Charlie. Even if he didn't do the right thing by you."

Owen's faith in her shouldn't have meant so much. As he'd just said, they barely knew each other. But relief flooded her nonetheless.

"I'm sorry I was suspicious of your motives at

first," he continued. "And I want you to know that I'm going to do whatever I can to make sure Charlie's friends here know you mean no harm."

"I'd appreciate that." Just as she couldn't help but appreciate the warmth of his touch.

"Are you up for hearing more about your father?"

Nodding, she said, "I do have one big question about him: Did he drink during the years you knew him?"

"No."

"He didn't?" She couldn't wrap her head around it. "I assumed that was the reason..." *The reason he never came back.*

Realizing Owen was waiting for her to continue, she decided there was no point in trying to keep it a secret any longer. "According to my mother," she explained, "Charlie was an alcoholic when they were married."

"I figured as much. Otherwise, it's likely he would have imbibed every now and again. But I never asked why he didn't drink. No one did, as far as I know. Is that why your mother and father split up?" he asked in a gentle voice. "Because of his drinking?"

"Partly."

She could keep holding her cards close to her chest. But then Owen would never truly understand why she hadn't seen her father in all this time, not unless she gave him the full, unvarnished truth.

And she found that she wanted to tell him. Somehow, she trusted him. Maybe it was the help he'd given her yesterday. Or maybe it was the way he was looking at her now—with understanding, but not pity. And with enough warmth that she almost felt like she was heating beneath his gaze.

"My mother had a job at an accounting firm in Santa Monica—the same one I work for now, actually. Charlie worked part time at a bookstore in the evenings so that he could take care of me during the day while my mom was at work. Even then, I think he dreamed of opening his own store. In any case, I was so young that I don't remember much, just snippets of having fun together playing conkers."

"That's a proper British game." Owen was clearly impressed. "Do you still play?"

"I haven't since he left." She took a sip of her drink before telling Owen the rest of it. "One day, he passed out and I left our apartment. The owner of the restaurant downstairs found me outside, about to cross a busy road by myself just as a truck came barreling down the street. I was three."

Owen looked shell-shocked.

"My mother kicked him out that night," Mari continued. "I don't know if he ever forgave himself—but my mom definitely hasn't. From that moment, she never wanted me to have anything to do with him…and he must have agreed, because he didn't want me again. One moment I had a father, the next I didn't. Even now, the bookstore isn't mine because he left it to me in his will. It's simply because I'm the only surviving blood relative the solicitors could track down."

"Guilt can turn people inside out," Owen noted in a low-pitched voice. "I'm sure the last thing Charlie wanted was to lose you. But…is it possible he didn't feel he deserved to be your father anymore?"

Mari wanted desperately to believe that explanation. Without proof that it was true, however, she just couldn't. "If he thought letting me run out into traffic was the worst thing he ever did, he was wrong. Walking out of my life forever was *far* worse."

"If I had known about you, and about what he did, I would have told him the same thing—that leaving you was wrong." Owen shook his head, still looking disturbed by her revelations. "I know that doesn't count for much now that it's too late."

"Actually, it does count. More than you know."

Mari looked down and realized their plates of food must have been delivered during their intense discussion. Her stomach felt tight and twisted, but knowing she had a lot of work ahead of her inside the bookstore, she made herself take a bite of her chickpea and avocado omelet. It was so delicious that her appetite magically made a resurgence.

"How did you come to manage your grandmother's business affairs?" she asked, hoping to take the spotlight off herself. "Was going into the family business always the plan?"

"As soon as I started at a tax law firm to finish my training, I realized I hated it. But after my parents had scrimped and saved for my education, sending me to the best schools, I couldn't stand the thought of letting them down. It wasn't until my grandmother threw me a lifeline and asked me to come on board with her book business that I felt I could step away from the law. Her previous manager had embezzled from her, and she wanted someone she could trust implicitly."

"Do you enjoy what you do now?"

"Very much. No day is ever the same, and once you meet her, you'll see why she always keeps me on my toes."

"Meet Mathilda Westcott?" Mari couldn't wrap her head around meeting one of her all-time-favorite authors. Then again, since Owen's grandmother and Charlie had been close, Mathilda would surely be another good person to speak to about him. "First thing I'm going to do when I get back to the store is find where Charlie kept the mysteries so that I can reread your grandmother's books."

"I've got meetings in Soho this afternoon, but I can come over tonight if you'd like some help."

Mari had thought she would be taking care of everything on her own. She'd never counted on meeting someone she would want to spill her guts to, who actually seemed to understand her reticence to accept her unexpected legacy, and who would be so willing to lend her a hand.

"I'd like that." A beam of sunlight crossed their table as they smiled at each other.

CHAPTER EIGHT

It seemed fitting to begin with the mysteries.

After all, there were two choices Mari could make right now. She could wash her hands of the bookstore and flat by passing them over to be sold by the solicitors, with whom she had just met, then head back to California. Or she could stay in England and try to run Elderflower Island Books as her own business.

Unfortunately, like all well-written mysteries, she couldn't for the life of her visualize the ending of the story.

Was it crazy of her to hope that perusing some of her favorite Mathilda Westcott novels could help her figure things out? Not only was Owen's grandmother a master at building plots that twisted and turned, she was also intimately familiar with the bookstore and island that provided their setting.

After breakfast, when Owen had headed to the train station to attend a meeting in central London, Mari had enough time to make a quick stop at the island's corner grocer before the solicitors came by the store for a meeting to discuss the details of her inheritance in person. The grocery was a surprisingly upscale place, with reclaimed wood shelves, organic produce, and baskets with mouthwatering home-baked scones and honeycombs. Given that the island's population couldn't be more than a few hundred people, Mari assumed there must be a large tourist population to support stores like this, the tea shop, and the boutiques.

Even on a weekday morning, there were plenty of people crossing the bridge with large cameras around their necks, or carrying walking sticks and wearing mud-encrusted hiking boots. Not to mention several people in neoprene carrying water shoes and blow-up paddle boards.

All around her, life moved forward. Tourists discovering a beautiful new part of the world. Locals appreciating their own waterways and parks.

And then there was Mari. A daughter who was only just beginning to discover who her absent father had been. *And* a woman who had been hit by an instant attraction—and connection—to Owen Sullivan.

She was looking forward to seeing Owen again tonight. But she was also nervous. Because falling for a charming Englishman was something her mother would *never* be able to accept. Even if Owen was nothing like Charlie.

In any case, Mari was getting way ahead of herself. Just because Owen had said she was pretty didn't mean they were going to launch a full-fledged love affair.

Besides, the meeting she'd just had with the solicitors had brought her down to earth. *Way* down. Inside the store, it was a relief to temporarily shove the legal and tax details of her inheritance into the back of her brain and turn her focus instead to the packed and untidy shelves.

Unsurprisingly, Charlie had stocked multiple copies of all twenty-five books in the *Bookshop on the River* series. Mari was in the middle of organizing Mathilda's books when she heard a knock on the door. Since Owen wasn't going to return until that evening, who was here to get a look at her now?

Wiping her dusty hands on her jeans, Mari went to open the door and found a pretty woman who looked to be in her mid-twenties standing outside.

"Hi, can I help you?"

"Actually, I was wondering if *I* could help *you*." The woman stuck out her hand. "I'm Alice Sullivan. You've met my brother Owen already." Alice's smile was totally genuine and disarming. As were the smudges of dirt on her face, hat, and clothes. "I'm not afraid to get dirty, as you can see, and I'm sure this feels like an awfully big job to tackle on your own."

Yesterday, Mari hadn't been sure that she wanted

anyone else involved in her mess. But Owen had been so kind—and spoken so warmly about his family—that she knew it would be a mistake to turn away his sister.

"Some help would be great. And please call me Mari." She stepped aside to let Alice in. "I'm working on the Mysteries section now. Any preference for which section you'd like to take a crack at organizing?"

"I work at Kew Gardens." She pointed in a westward direction. "It's only a five-minute bus ride away if you want to come for a personal tour. Which is my long-winded way of saying I would be happy to dig into the gardening section. Charlie always had a nice selection of titles, but I'll admit I wished I could have taken charge of his shelving decisions."

"Considering I don't know a primrose from a peony, I'd be delighted for you to have at it."

Mysteries and Gardening were close enough for the two women to chat as they took books off the shelves, dusted, then reshelved the books in their proper places.

"How are you liking England so far?" Alice asked.

"I love it as much as I thought I would. Even more, actually."

"I'm really glad to hear that. But I'm so sorry you couldn't come under happier circumstances. We all miss your father."

"I didn't really know him." Mari had barely spoken of her father for most of her life. But now that she was in his home, she couldn't keep the words from spilling out. At least when it came to the Sullivans. Though she didn't know what Owen had told his sister, she suspected he wasn't much for gossip. "He left when I was three."

"I had no idea." Alice leaned away from the shelf she was reorganizing so that Mari could see her face. "You must have really mixed feelings about being here—and not just because it's such a mess."

"I do." Mari appreciated the way Alice immediately understood. "Although today is a lot better than yesterday."

"Good. And hopefully, tomorrow will be even better than today." With that, she tucked back into the Gardening shelves.

Mari liked Alice—her sunny outlook, her honest and straight-to-the-point emotional responses, her willingness to pitch in. "Owen said he was one of five. Do your siblings all live close by?"

"Everyone is in London, but we don't see much of Fiona. We haven't seen much of Owen for the last year either," she added.

What had happened a year ago in Owen's life? Mari wondered. Had he also been hit with a massive life change from out of the blue, just like her?

"Has my brother already given you the family rundown, or should I?" Alice asked.

"I know your names and, of course I'm a huge fan of your grandmother's books, but I'd love to hear more." Learning about the people Charlie had been close to made Mari feel a little closer to him.

"Okay." Mari could hear the smile in Alice's voice as she began to run through the details of her family. "If you didn't already know, Owen is the oldest and in charge of running Gran's business. He works *all* the time. His office is just down the road in Gran's cottage, where she's probably sitting at her desk in the window right now, working on her next novel. Malcolm is next oldest and does big business deals. Then there's Tom and his little girl, Aria. She's five and the most beautiful angel you'll ever see." Alice was full of pure love for her niece. "Tom puts on concerts all over England. Pop, rock, jazz, classical—pretty much whatever takes his fancy. There's a venue on the island that we've been trying to convince him to take over. The Rolling Stones, The Who, and tons of other bands got their start there. The concert hall is starting to crumble from years of neglect, unfortunately, but I'm thinking if he took it over, he and Aria could move to the island for good."

"What about his wife?"

Alice snorted from the other side of the shelves. "Don't get me started. Tom and Aria's mother never married—which wasn't at all a bad thing. Especially since she barely stuck around long enough to give birth. I *really* hope you don't like Lyla Imogen's songs."

"Your brother has a daughter with *Lyla Imogen*?"

"It was before she was famous. He's the one who gave her her big break. Anyway, then there's my sister, Fiona. With her fancy house in Chelsea and all her couture gowns for the charity events she chairs, everything looks perfect on the surface. But I'm not sure she's happy. Especially with her husband, Lewis."

Hearing about Owen and Alice's family made Mari realize she wasn't the only one with a complicated life story.

"You're not afraid to tell it like it is, are you?" Mari had never met anyone quite like Alice, someone who held nothing back and expected the same from others.

"It's always easier to diagnose someone else's problems, rather than look at your own," Alice replied. "At least that's what my mum always tells me."

"Are your parents close by too?"

"They're just across the river in St. Margarets. I'll take you exploring, if you like." She leaned back so that Mari could see her sparkling eyes as she added, "Unless Owen beats me to it."

"He's been really nice and helpful." Mari tried, and failed, to hide her blush. "Tell me more about your parents."

"Mum puts on exhibitions at the V&A. We grew

up running around the museum after hours."

"From what I've read online, the Victoria & Albert Museum looks incredible."

"There are so many places in London you've got to see. I know some people think the city is dirty and crowded, but I love it!"

"I do too, at least from the little I've seen so far."

"Charlie also loved London." Alice paused. "Is it okay for me to talk about him?"

"Actually, it's a bit of a relief." Mari was surprised to realize how true that was. "Coming here isn't only about figuring out if I should reopen his store—it's also about learning who he was. Tell me, what did he love about London?"

"Charlie was fascinated by the history of the Underground. My dad was a train engineer for a long time, so they always bonded over Tube trivia."

"Your father drove trains on the London Underground?" Mari marveled. "I can't think of a more quintessentially British job, other than guarding Buckingham Palace."

"If you really want British tradition, you should come for our big Sunday roast this weekend. I know my parents would love to meet you. Malc will probably talk your ear off about the year he lived in the States." Before Mari could reply, Alice jumped up from her stool. "Oh! I've been talking so much that I almost forgot to pick up the cosmos seeds I need from Petersham Nurseries. Sorry I wasn't more help. I'll swing back as soon as I get another free moment. I'd love to tackle the patio garden in the back next time, if you'd like?"

"You have no idea how much I would appreciate that. It seems like such a big job for a nongreen thumb like me that I was tempted to ignore it for the time being."

"Don't worry, I'll make it beautiful for you and your customers. I have some extra plants that I can't squeeze into my own tiny garden, so I'll bring those with me next time. And if you're up for it, either Owen or I will come by to take you to our parents' house on Sunday."

Alice Sullivan was a whirlwind, in the best way possible. If Mari could channel only half her energy, she'd be done sorting out the bookstore in no time.

As the bookstore door closed behind the other woman, Mari took a step back to look at their progress. Now, two shelves in each section they'd worked on looked perfect. Though it might not be much progress in the grand scheme of things, at the very least it gave her a sense of how the store could look once all the shelves were dusted and put into good order.

Her accountant's brain guesstimated there were approximately two hundred and fifty shelves in the store. At a half hour cleanup time per shelf, that was three forty-hour weeks put into nothing but shelf cleanup and reorganization. Who knew how much time it would take to take care of everything else, like painting and creating a website and ordering new inventory? Still, she'd never been afraid of hard work before. Just because this particular business and location and connection to her father had a tendency to send her emotions topsy-turvy didn't negate her work ethic.

The buzzing in her pocket interrupted her thoughts. Pulling out her phone, she saw Carson's face on the screen. She clicked to accept the video call. "Hi."

"Hey, sis. How's England so far?"

"England is amazing." Knowing he would see the truth in her face, she didn't bother trying to spin anything. "The store, on the other hand…" She did a slow scan of the room so he could see it.

He let out a low whistle. "That looks pretty daunting."

"I've just calculated that it's going to take me three weeks just to clean up the shelves. But I've decided there's no use in panicking about it, when the best thing I can do is just get on with it."

"I like your positive outlook," he said, "and I know you wanted to tackle this on your own, but—"

"I'm not on my own. I seem to have been semi-adopted by a couple of members of a local family who were close to Charlie. They've both been in to help already, and I've been invited to have a roast lunch with them this Sunday."

"After the way Mom talked about your birth father our whole lives, it's a little strange to think that he had close friends, isn't it?"

She nodded. "I keep thinking that if he wasn't such a bad guy after all, then why did he never reach out to me? I mean, maybe it was harder when I was still a kid and he knew how angry Mom was. But once I was an adult, he could have at least held out an olive branch."

"Mari." Carson's voice was gentle. "Whatever his reasons were for abandoning you, none of them have been your fault. No matter what you find out while you're in England, that fact won't change."

From a purely rational standpoint, she knew her brother was right. And if her life was nothing more than a spreadsheet, the way she kept trying to force it to be every time she felt overwhelmed, rational would win every time.

But emotion rarely ran along rational lines, did it?

"Thanks for checking in," she said, giving him a small smile. "How are things going for you?"

"Crazy, like always." He ran a hand through his hair, which was sticking straight up. Given the time difference, she guessed he had only just gotten out of bed. "But family comes first, so if you ever get to a point where you need serious backup, promise you'll call me."

"I will." Sunlight was streaming in the window. Before they hung up, she wanted her brother to see some of the reasons why she wasn't willing to turn away from the hard work of putting the store back together, no matter how daunting the task. "I've shown you the mess. Now I'm going to show you the beauty." Walking outside, she did another slow scan with her phone, this time of the river, the pub, the street as it wound down to the boathouse, then the other way toward the boutiques and corner grocer. "Isn't it *incredible?*"

"It couldn't look more different than SoCal—and it couldn't look more like *you*." He grinned. "You're going to knock this out of the park, Mari." It was what she always said to him when he was going in for yet another important pitch meeting for his startup. And she had been right every time. "Something tells me Elderflower Island is where you're meant to be."

No matter how badly she might secretly wish it was true, she wasn't one hundred percent sure yet. Especially if she couldn't get the bookstore up and running at a profit before the money ran out. And that wasn't accounting for how furious her mother would be if she *did* end up staying.

They hung up, and as Mari slipped the phone back into her pocket, she filled her lungs with fresh air. Yes, she remained confused as to why her father had behaved as he had. Yes, she was pretty darn far out of her comfort zone in running a bookstore—especially one that needed so much work before she could even reopen it. But it was one of her biggest dreams to own a bookstore. And right now, that seemed more important than anything else.

Fueled with new determination, she headed back into the store and threw herself into cleaning and organizing the next shelf.

CHAPTER NINE

Rush hour on the Tube was a crush, as always. Tonight, however, Owen was too preoccupied with thoughts of Mari to pay the crowd much mind.

He nearly laughed out loud at himself. Talk about a *crush*—he was acting more like a fifteen-year-old schoolboy than a thirty-six-year-old man. There was just something about Charlie's daughter.

She was beautiful, but in an utterly unique way.

She had been hurt, but she wasn't at all broken.

She had been sent into a difficult situation, but still seemed full of hope.

Hope. It was such a fragile thing, yet so damned important.

Owen would never forget the night he'd found Mathilda lying unconscious on the floor of her cottage. Calling 999, he'd hoped with everything he had that she would be okay, that she would recover, that he wouldn't lose one of the most important people in his life.

A year on, her doctors agreed she was in fine form.

She had made brilliant strides on all fronts, from speaking to writing to walking. Everything he'd hoped for had come to pass. And yet, he still worried about her.

The conductor's voice broke through his thoughts, alerting passengers that the Richmond station was the end of the District Line and to please disembark. Today, there had been good service on the line, so Owen had made it home from central London in little more than a half hour. Funneling out of the station alongside hundreds of strangers, he was glad for the walk down the high street to stretch his legs.

Soon, he was on Elderflower Island and letting himself into his grandmother's cottage. When he couldn't find her at her writing table, in the living room, or in the kitchen, he called, "Gran?"

He'd texted her several times throughout the day to make sure all was well, but he still held his breath, waiting for her response. Despite the immense progress she'd made, he couldn't shake the fear that he would return one day and find her on the kitchen floor again. It was why he had kept his outings to a bare minimum for the past year.

"Hello, darling." His grandmother came into the kitchen, holding a basket of newly dug-up potatoes from the kitchen garden, her cheeks rosy from the sunshine and exertion. "How were your meetings in town?"

"Excellent." He breathed a silent sigh of relief that she was okay. "The special holiday editions are coming along nicely." He put the bag he'd carried home on the counter. "I picked up Chelsea buns from that baker you like on Archer Street in Soho."

"Always so thoughtful." She gave him a kiss on his cheek. "Now, you had better get ready for your date."

He raised an eyebrow. "I don't believe Mari would call it that." It didn't go unnoticed by either of them that he wasn't disputing the word *date* on his own behalf. Truthfully, he wouldn't have minded if it was a date.

"Poor thing is probably too overwhelmed by everything that has happened. Come to think of it," she added, her eyes twinkling, "you look a little overwhelmed too."

He had to laugh at her obvious delight in his reaction to Charlie's daughter. "Sorry to disappoint, Gran, especially when we all know just how good your imagination is, but tonight will likely come to nothing more than eating Chinese takeaway and helping her give the rugs in the bookshop a good hoovering."

"Whatever the two of you end up doing together, I'm pleased to see you going out. I've lived a full and wonderful life—it's time for you to go live yours."

"You've still got plenty of time left, Gran."

"I know that." She shooed him out of the room. "Which is why I'm kicking you out to go charm the knickers off the island's newest resident."

Only Mathilda Westcott would be so blatant about her intentions for Owen and Mari, all the way down to her more lascivious hopes for them, knickers and all.

God love her. He couldn't imagine a world without his grandmother in it.

★ ★ ★

Elderflower Island wasn't large, but its residents certainly didn't lack for the necessities. Chinese takeaway was on Owen's must-have list, and Sue Yang's kitchen never disappointed.

Sue was bagging up the food when he walked in. "Hello, Owen." She gestured to his larger-than-normal order. "Is your family visiting tonight?"

This was the perfect chance to start getting the news out around the island that Mari was not only no threat to anyone, but the more locals who rallied around her, the better.

"Charlie's daughter is here," he told Sue as he paid. "I'm taking dinner over to the bookshop, then helping her with whatever she needs done to get it back up and running. She's a really nice person, and I'd like to see her succeed." He lifted the bag. "I'm sure she's going to love your food, Sue. Cheers."

Just that quickly, the underground island news network would start humming into overdrive.

Owen was humming too as he headed down the street to Elderflower Island Books. He couldn't remember the last time he'd felt like this. Walking with a new spring in his step, under a clear sky, surrounded by flowers that had never smelled quite so fragrant. It wasn't simply that the past year had been overshadowed by worries about his grandmother.

It was more a feeling that whatever he'd been waiting for his whole life was finally here.

He knocked on the bookshop door. Through the window, he saw Mari turn. A smile lit her face—the same smile he knew was mirrored on his face.

"Hi." She looked a little shy as she opened the door and let him in. Until she smelled dinner, that was. "That smells *amazing*." She put a hand over her stomach at the same moment it let out a loud growl. "I got into such a groove here that I forgot to eat lunch."

"I thought that might happen, so I ordered loads."

"How about we go up to the flat and eat in the kitchen you so thoughtfully cleaned yesterday?"

As they headed for the stairs, he took a look around the shop—and was, frankly, astonished by everything she'd already accomplished. The shelves facing the door were dust-free and organized, the piles of books that had littered the floor and seats had been cleared away, and the floor had been polished. "You did all this by yourself?"

"Your sister Alice came by to help." Mari smiled. "She's great."

"She is," he agreed. But he also knew that Alice likely hadn't been able to stay long, probably only the length of her lunch break. "You must be exhausted." Between the hard work and jet lag, Mari was likely about to drop.

"Actually, I feel surprisingly good. I just kept telling myself to 'keep calm and carry on cleaning.'" She let them into the flat, then went to refill and turn on the kettle. She might have spent only one night in Britain, but her tea-making instincts were that of a native. Over her shoulder, she said, "The queen would probably have my head for butchering the iconic phrase, wouldn't she?"

"On the contrary," he said, "I think she'd be pleased by your stiff upper lip."

Mari got out plates and silverware while he unloaded cartons of kung pao chicken, chow mein, mu shu pork, egg rolls, and steamed rice onto the kitchen table.

"Did Charlie have that?" she asked. "A stiff upper lip, I mean."

Her tone was mild, and she didn't stop laying the table. But her surface nonchalance couldn't disguise how much Owen's answers about Charlie's life and personality meant to her. He got the sense she was mentally sliding into place one small puzzle piece after another in the hopes that one day, she would finally be able to see a full picture of the father she'd barely known.

"He definitely did," Owen replied. "I never heard him complain about anything."

She met his eyes across the table. "It's one thing never to complain—it's another entirely to be truly happy." The words were barely out of her mouth when she waved her hand in the air as if to erase them. "I swore I wasn't going to pin you to the wall with a hundred and one questions about Charlie the second you walked in."

"When I said I'm happy to try to answer any questions you have about him, I meant it. And as to whether or not he was happy? My grandmother would probably know better than any of us, but despite how close they were, I'm not sure how much he opened up even to her."

"Did she know about me?"

"I'm pretty sure she was the only one here who did. But she never told a soul. Whatever Charlie said to her went into the vault and has stayed there. Now that you're here, however, I wouldn't be surprised to find that she's willing to talk to you directly."

Mari shook her head. "I wouldn't want her to feel that she's betraying his confidences. Everyone needs someone they can trust to hold their deepest, darkest secrets."

I want to be the one to hold yours.

He nearly said the words aloud. But it would only frighten her away if she knew the impact she'd already had on him. If she had any sense of how much he wanted to protect her. Help her.

Kiss her.

"I don't imagine many people would feel that way," he said in a low voice, unable to look away from her lips. Unable to keep from imagining how it would feel to have her in his arms.

And to taste her.

"We should be able to trust the people we love. And," she added with a little smile that made his heart beat even faster, "you should be able to come here and eat Chinese food without having a philosophical discussion about trust and secret-keeping."

Owen would have been perfectly happy to continue their conversation—he'd never gone so deep, so fast, with anyone before—but this was clearly her cue to move away from talking about her father for the time being.

She made tea with the green tea bags Sue had supplied. Bringing the teapot over to the table, along with two mugs, she said, "I'd love to hear about your experiences growing up here. All the buildings have such amazing history that I can't help but think it must have been like living in a Harry Potter novel."

He waited until she'd served herself before he filled his own plate. "One look at my secondary school would only serve to confirm your suspicions that all British kids live in a J. K. Rowling novel." He spoke around bites of food. Mari, meanwhile, was devouring the mu shu pork. "The campus comes complete with stone gargoyles at the gate."

"Seriously?"

He pulled out his phone and showed her a photo of his school on the Internet. "Seriously."

She raised an eyebrow as she moved on to the shrimp fried rice. "You're not going to whip out a wand and cast a spell over me, are you?"

He laughed. "Believe me, if I could cast a spell to get the shop and flat organized as quickly and painlessly as possible, I would." When a shadow fell across her face at the reminder of how much work was ahead of her, he quickly pivoted back to talking about his childhood. "As I told you before, my parents' sacrifices for me are why I nearly continued with tax law—I felt I owed it to them and shouldn't chuck it in after all they'd done to help me get the degree."

"Believe me," she said, "I get it. It's a big part of

why I'm so torn over inheriting the flat and bookstore. My mom and stepfather have always been there for me. They've given me anything I needed. A great home. The chance to go to an excellent university, then take on a challenging job at the accounting firm. Choosing to come here—to consider staying in England—feels like a betrayal. To put it mildly, Mom isn't thrilled that I'm here." She twirled a few chow mein noodles on her fork, but didn't make a move to actually eat them. "If you don't mind my asking, how did your parents react once you left the law to work for your grandmother? I'm sure they were happy you were helping her, but did you ever get the sense they were disappointed by what you'd left behind?"

"It was the exact opposite. When they saw how much happier I was working with Gran, they apologized for not steering me toward something more fulfilling much earlier. In the same way that I didn't want to diminish their sacrifices, they hadn't wanted to diminish my achievements by suggesting I quit. We had been running circles around each other for years, when what we really wanted was for one another to be happy." He held her gaze. "I know your mother's relationship with Charlie was complicated, but I can't imagine she would want to keep you from your happy ending. Or beginning, as the case may be."

"Can I tell you a secret?" She licked her lips, drawing his gaze back to her mouth.

"You can tell me anything, Mari."

"Owning a bookstore is my dream come true." Her eyes sparkled with passion as she said, "I *love* books. The way they smell and feel and the endless worlds and possibilities and joy and dreams between the covers. I still can't believe I've inherited a bookstore. Even today, when I was practically buried in dust, it was *glorious*. And the truth is that despite knowing how upset my mom is about my being in her ex-husband's home—" She looked around the flat, which had easily two hundred books on shelves, side tables, and windowsills. "I love being surrounded by Charlie's books. And though I know it's crazy, I can't help but think one of the gazillion books in this building is going to help steer me in the right direction in the end."

"It's not crazy, Mari. Nothing you're saying is." At the same time, he knew all too well the toll guilt took on you—and he hated the idea of Mari falling into that dark hole. "Tell me what I can help you with tonight that will lessen your load. So that you can see things more clearly."

"You've already done so much. I know how loyal you were to Charlie, and I think it's absolutely lovely that he had dear friends like you, but that doesn't mean you need to bend over backward to help me when you have your own life to lead."

"Right now, this is exactly where my life has led me. To *you*." He let his words take root before adding, "I like you, Mari. And not only because you're my friend's daughter."

* * *

Two days ago, Mari had been in her Santa Monica office taking care of last-minute emails. Tonight, she was sitting in Charlie's Elderflower Island flat, above the bookstore she now owned, while an absolutely gorgeous Englishman looked at her with such heat in his eyes...

Could this really be her life? Could she be brave enough to admit—not only to Owen, but also to herself—that she felt the same way he did?

Barely twenty-four hours after meeting him, she felt the butterflies in her stomach flying faster and faster. And she couldn't stop wondering how it would feel to press her lips, and her body, against his.

As though he could read her mind, he lowered his gaze to her mouth. Without thinking, she put her fingertips to her lips, tingling now from nothing more than the heat of his gaze.

Belatedly realizing what she'd done, she pulled her hand away and cleared her throat. "I like you too." Her words were barely more than a whisper. "But everything is already so topsy-turvy..."

"I'm your friend, first and foremost," he reassured her. "No matter what else does or doesn't happen between us, that isn't going to change."

She'd never realized how sexy kindness could be until tonight. A few more sweet words from Owen and she was liable to launch herself into his arms.

It wasn't at all easy to stop herself from doing just that—or to remind herself that just as she tackled her client accounts with methodical precision, she should deal with the bookstore first. Once she knew what she was doing with it, then she could look harder at her feelings for Owen.

"Thank you." She wanted to reach for his hand, but touching him would only set her heart racing again and the butterflies flying. Though she'd always thought that being methodical about everything was a good idea, at the moment she couldn't quite remember why.... "Knowing I have a friend here, it helps so much. And your cleaning the fridge yesterday was pretty high up there on my list of awesome too. I don't know many guys who would have been brave enough to tackle the mess."

"My mum is the one to thank for that. She was a firm believer that her sons should excel at housework as much as sports or playing video games. All the more reason for you to tell me what's next on your cleanup list." Before she could protest that he must have better things to do with his time, he added, "My grandmother insisted on a night to herself at the cottage. Which means I'm yours for the duration, if you want me."

She couldn't keep the flush her cheeks at his words: *I'm yours.* Her blush grew even hotter at the realization of just how badly she wanted him, despite trying to be rational about dealing with a ton of massive life changes and upheavals.

"What's the most difficult task on your to-do list?" he prompted again while she worked to push away the longing, and the desire, welling up inside her.

At least this question was an easy one. Because while she was happy with the progress she'd made in the bookstore today, the truth was that she was still avoiding the hard stuff. "I haven't been in Charlie's room yet," she admitted. "Maybe we could go through his things together?"

"Sounds good. And remember, once we're in there, if you need a breather at any point—or just want to call a halt for the night—we can always just go across to the pub for a drink."

"It's tempting to chuck it in and go now," she admitted. "But all these years, I had so many questions. Now that I'm here, I need to face whatever answers I get. Good or bad."

They were standing at the sink, close enough for him to reach for her hand. "You're a very brave woman, Mari."

"I don't know if I ever was before," she told him in a low voice. "But now...here...I want to be brave." She wanted it so badly, in fact, that she needed to prove it by taking a step forward instead of back. And then another. And another. Until she was close enough to Owen to see the flecks of gold in his blue eyes. "I want to be brave enough to ask if I can kiss you."

Heat surged between them as he replied, "Kiss me, Mari."

CHAPTER TEN

Owen's five-o'clock shadow was rough against Mari's palm. His body was lean and strong against hers. And his eyes simmered with barely quenched desire as she went to her tippy-toes and pressed her lips, ever so softly, against his.

The kiss was barely more than a breath.

And yet it was *everything*.

She lowered her hand from his cheek, but before she could step back, Owen slipped his arm around her waist, holding her against him.

His blue eyes were dark with hunger. And when Owen looked at her this way, Mari couldn't help but feel like her dreams just might be within reach after all…

She had to kiss him again, threading her hands into his dark hair and letting her passions run free and wild for a few blissful moments.

When they finally let each other go, she had a choice to make. She could worry that they were moving too fast. She could let guilt take her over for so much as considering dating an Englishman.

Or she could simply let all of that go for the moment and smile at the gorgeous man holding her in his arms.

When her lips turned up at the corners, so did his. "My grandmother is going to be so pleased."

Wholly caught off guard, she asked, "How so?"

"As soon as she heard you were coming," he said as he brushed a lock of hair from her face, "I suspect she started writing a grand romance inside her head."

A grand romance. There were few things Mari enjoyed reading about more. True love written in the stars. Couples fated to be together, no matter the barriers. Breathless passion that only grew richer with time.

And yet, she'd never thought it could happen to her. Not until this moment, when she kissed a handsome man she'd met barely a day ago in a flat, above a bookstore, on an island in the River Thames in England.

Reeling not only from the kiss, but also from all the outer *and* inner changes taking place in her life, she suddenly needed a little space to think more clearly. She reluctantly moved out of his arms. "Do you tell your grandmother about every woman you kiss?"

"I never have before. But I don't think she'll need me to say anything. She'll take one look at me and know."

Mari was almost afraid to ask. "Know what?"

"That I'm captivated by you. Captivated enough that I'm not willing to risk coming on too fast. No matter how much I want to." Which explained why, instead of reaching for her again, he simply smiled and said, "What do you say we head into Charlie's room and get started?"

She nodded, grateful for the way Owen understood her need to process what had happened—and that he hadn't taken offense. Especially given that she'd been the one to kiss him first. Other men might have felt that she'd led them on, but Mari could tell that he would never think that.

Leaving the kitchen, they headed down the short hallway. Mari put her hand on Charlie's bedroom doorknob and paused, her chest clenching tight. She'd never imagined she would be the one to go through her father's things after his death. But she'd just proved that she was braver than she thought, hadn't she? She could be brave again.

What's more, a few minutes ago, when she'd said to Owen, *"It's one thing to never complain—it's another entirely to be truly happy,"* she hadn't been talking only about Charlie. She'd also been talking about herself.

At last, she wasn't merely ready to be happy, she was willing to do whatever it took to find joy. Even if some of those things felt truly terrifying…

Turning the knob, she pushed open the door. The surfaces were cluttered and dusty, but after spending the day working in Charlie's bookstore, she understood that it was an organized chaos. He had tended to group things by use. The stack of old shoelaces with the cans of leather polish. A half-dozen reading glasses with different-colored frames. Clippings from newspapers tacked to a board on the wall. And of course, the books stacked absolutely everywhere, whether at the end of the bed or propping open the closet door.

"What do you want to go through first?" Owen asked. "There's a charity shop on the island that I'm sure would be happy to take whatever clothes and shoes you would like to donate."

She appreciated Owen's gentle nudge out of her head. "Great idea. Anything in good condition, let's stack on the bed. Anything we're going to toss, let's put in a pile by the window to bag up later."

Owen had already begun taking shoes out of the closet by the time she steeled herself to open Charlie's top dresser drawer. Holding her breath at what she might find inside, relief washed through her when she saw nothing more than a stack of white undershirts.

"At dinner," she said, "you told me a little about growing up here. I'd love to hear more."

"I grew up in St. Margarets," Owen told her, "just

across the river from Richmond. Property values have skyrocketed, but when I was growing up, it was simply a nice family neighborhood on the outskirts of London. I went to the local primary until I was eleven and then, as I mentioned at breakfast, on to Hogwarts for senior school."

More glad than she could say that she was able to laugh while going through her father's things, she asked, "Were you sporty?"

"I played cricket and rugby. Broke a couple of bones, but what kid doesn't?"

She hadn't, because her mother had always encouraged her to stay away from the riskier sports. Tennis and swimming had been allowed, rather than lacrosse or soccer. All her life, her mother had done her utmost to keep her safe, as though she was forever trying to make up for what had nearly happened that day on Third Street.

Shaking herself out of her thoughts yet again, she said, "There's a rugby ground in Twickenham, isn't there?"

He nodded. "My dad never misses an England game. You'll have to come with us."

As she took a stack of socks out of the second drawer and put them in the discard pile, she couldn't help but hear the part of the sentence he'd left off: *If you're still here.*

"Alice said your father drove trains for the Tube. That must have been hugely exciting for a little boy."

"Everyone wanted to come to my sixth birthday party for a chance to sit behind the wheel of the train." She could hear the smile in his voice as he spoke about his father—the same joy that resounded whenever he talked about his family. "Now Dad works with the drivers, training them on new systems, making sure they're getting enough sleep, and convincing them to go to counseling even when they insist they don't need it."

She looked up from the bottom drawer, about to ask why the drivers would need counseling, when it dawned on her that people sometimes stepped onto the tracks—either deliberately or by accident. "I didn't even think about the things your father must have seen."

"We always knew something bad had happened at work on the nights when he sat at the dinner table without touching his food. He was there, but he wasn't, if that makes any sense. Mum is the one who convinced him to see someone to talk about it."

"Your mom sounds amazing."

"She is." He took a stack of long-sleeved shirts from the closet and laid them on the bed to sort. "I spoke with her this afternoon during my commute home. She'd like to have you 'round for Sunday roast. Alice also said she'd mentioned it to you. Will you come?"

It was one thing to work on putting the bookstore to rights—even to reopen it, since it would probably be best to have it operational if Mari wanted to sell it for the best price. It was yet another to kiss Owen. But going to lunch with his family felt even bigger. As though she was setting down roots, making friends, building a future here.

No wonder her mother hadn't wanted her to come to Elderflower Island. Donna must have known that the pull to stay might very well end up being stronger than Mari's willingness to return to a life in Southern California that was good, but miles from everything she dreamed of.

Out of solidarity with her mother and stepfather, she should make her excuses about having lunch with Owen's family. Only, how could she resist a man who adored his grandmother so much that he had devoted his career to building her business? Who happily talked on the phone with his mother? Who had brought Mari fresh jam and scones made by his sister? *And* whose kisses made her breathless?

"I would love to spend Sunday with your family. Thank you."

Flustered by how she was managing to get in deeper and deeper with Owen with every moment that passed, she opened the lowest drawer of the dresser without pausing to prepare herself first for what she might find inside.

Her breath caught at the sight of a small, pink dress. A tiny sweater. A pair of white ankle socks printed with red hearts. Everything in the drawer would fit a three-year-old.

As the initial shock subsided, Mari recognized the clothes from photos in her mother's old albums as those she had worn as a child.

She sat back on her heels and put her hand over the ache in her chest.

"Mari?" Owen stopped taking shirts off hangers and came to her side. "What did you find?"

With trembling hands, she lifted the little dress from the drawer. "This was mine. The sweater and socks were too. He must have taken them when he left California." A tear fell, and then another, even though she was smiling too. Joy and sorrow seemed intrinsically bound together whenever she thought of her father. "All this time, I thought he forgot about me. Or just didn't care. But after finding these clothes and the book this morning—"

"What book?"

"*Winnie-the-Pooh*. It was my favorite bedtime story. He would read it to me every night. When you came to the door this morning, I had just found a signed first edition." She gathered the dress to her chest. "It was almost as though he left it there for me to find."

As Owen's arms came around her, despite her tears, she realized relief had also taken hold. Relief at finding out in yet another way that she *had* mattered to her father.

She'd never stop wishing that she could have seen him while he was alive. That she could have talked with him. Touched his hand one more time. But if this was all she could have, she would take it. And she would be grateful for the small sense of peace she could now hold onto whenever she thought about her father from this moment forward.

She lifted her head from Owen's shoulder. "Thank you for being here. For helping."

He brushed the wetness from her cheeks. "He would have been so proud of you, Mari. So damned proud."

She inhaled a shaky breath, realizing for the first time that it might actually be true.

In the aftermath of the emotional upheaval, exhaustion swept over her. She yawned, so big her jaw made a small popping noise. "I think it's officially past my bedtime." She got to her feet, her knees a little wobbly. "Thank you for helping me make a start in here."

"It was my pleasure."

She walked him downstairs and through the bookstore. As soon as she opened the door, the black cat came sauntering in and leaped up on the counter by the register to settle in for the night.

"Do you know the cat's name?" she asked.

"Charlie always called him Mars. I'm assuming because his coloring makes him look like the candy bar, with the nougat and caramel on the inside and milk chocolate on the outside."

Mari was momentarily speechless. "That was his nickname for me. *Mars.*" But even that discovery couldn't keep her from yawning again.

"Don't forget, anything you need—even if it's just a spoonful of sugar for your tea—I'm close by at Gran's. Her cottage is at 386 Elderflower Lane."

"Even the addresses in England sound like they've come from a fairy tale," Mari murmured, so sleepy suddenly that she almost felt as though she were already dreaming.

He smiled at her random statement. "Do you need help with anything else before I go?"

"Just this." She wrapped her arms around his waist and rested her cheek on his chest, the steady beat of his heart lulling her even further.

And when he squeezed her back, she wondered if maybe the first edition *Winnie-the-Pooh* hadn't been the only gift her father had left for her.

Because she would be very lucky indeed to get to call Charlie's friends her own.

Especially a man who just might end up being so much more than a friend.

CHAPTER ELEVEN

Mari woke early the next morning, filled with a renewed sense of purpose after having found yet more proof last night that Charlie hadn't forgotten her. While she still didn't understand why he had never tried to make contact with her when she was a teenager or an adult, it meant a great deal to her to now know for certain that she had been important to him as a child. Important enough to keep reminders of her through *Winnie-the-Pooh*, his cat, and her baby clothes in his bottom dresser drawer.

She decided to take a quick bath before starting her day in the store. Who was she kidding—clawfoot-tub soaks weren't meant to be *quick*. After luxuriating in the bubbles until the water grew cold, she dressed, then headed into the kitchen to turn on the kettle for a cup of tea and turn on the range to make oatmeal...then promptly forgot about both while staring out the window, daydreaming about Owen Sullivan.

Last night, she'd dreamed plenty about him too—dreamed of his kisses, of how good it felt when he held her. She'd come to Elderflower Island hoping to learn about Charlie's life, but she'd found that and so much more. Wonder and beauty and friendly people.

And, most unexpectedly of all, Owen.

The whistle of the kettle and the smell of burning oats snapped her back to reality. One where she needed to head downstairs to dive back into piles of books and dust. Would she uncover any unexpected treasures today? Previously, she had been cautiously hopeful.

This morning, she could no longer hold hope back.

Mars the cat stretched when she entered the bookstore, his fur rising in a black wave from front to back as he woke up. In her search of the cupboards upstairs, she'd found a stock of cans of wet cat food. Opening one, she poured it into a bowl. In another bowl, she poured water from the bottle she'd clipped on the belt loop of her jeans. Though Mars gave the bowls a cursory sniff and taste after he hopped down from the counter, he soon headed for the door. Not at all surprised that better spoils awaited him at the pub, Mari let him out.

It was another gloriously beautiful day. The river sparkled in the sunlight, the grass and trees were brilliantly green, and people went about their business with smiles on their faces. A man in a white apron stopped sweeping leaves outside the pub to smile and wave at her. Smiling and waving back, she decided today would be a good day to venture out for lunch and meet a few of the island locals. After all, if she did decide to stay in London, she hoped to be a part of the community.

Her heart skipped a beat at the thought. She would need to gather more financial data about the viability of the bookstore as a profitable business before she could make any firm decisions, of course. But barring massive disaster, she had begun to think that staying might not be as impossible as she'd once believed.

A retro-style radio sat on the shelf behind the register, and she turned it on. It was playing Chopin, and after *Prelude in E Minor* concluded, the announcer thanked listeners for supporting Classic FM.

It felt like yet another insight into her father's life. He had liked classical music. So did she.

Though Mari didn't have a musical bone in her body, she'd always been struck by how powerful music could be for evoking not only emotions, but also vivid mental pictures. With Haydn playing now, and sun streaming in the windows, she could see the bookstore as it might have been while her father was behind the register ringing up a purchase, or climbing on one of the shelf ladders to locate the perfect book for a customer. She could see someone curled up on the tweed armchair in the corner, thumbing through one of the gardening books Alice had so carefully shelved. A mother and child on the rug in the kids' section reading a picture book together. A mystery lovers' book group meeting in the alcove next to Mathilda Westcott's books, sharing recommendations for new authors and series to explore next. A guest author reading from her new bestseller to a crowd of happy fans.

Picturing the bookstore in all its glory put a smile on Mari's face as she tackled the children's section. According to her mother, she'd been a voracious reader practically from birth. The only thing they'd ever really fought about, in fact, was how often Mari had been caught reading with a flashlight under the covers, hours past her bedtime.

All Mari's life, books had been the one thing she could count on, going as far back as three years old, when her world had turned on a dime—not only losing her father, but living with a mother who alternated between fury and tears, strength and fragility.

Nothing calmed Mari faster than a book. Nothing cheered her to higher heights than a book. Nothing brought her as much knowledge as a book.

She loved the idea of curating a children's section that could do the same for local kids. A place to feel comfortable, no matter where you came from, how much money you had, or whether your parents or friends liked to read. Of course, she understood that she would need to make a profit if she intended to run the store, but if she did end up keeping the business, at least one part of the store would never have to make sense on a spreadsheet of pluses and minuses. The children's section would be purely about fun and joy and inspiration. Even if that one area of the store ran at a financial loss, giving a child a reason to smile and dream and be curious was so much more important.

Feeling lighter than she had in a long while, Mari emptied shelves of children's stories, wiped them down, dusted books, then reorganized them, first grouping together her favorite authors, then shelving everything else in alphabetical order.

Yesterday while she'd been working, her lingering worries had still been dragging her down. Today, she couldn't remember when she'd ever been happier to work on something.

Okay, so everything was still pretty much up in the air, given that she still needed to have a serious look at the bookstore's financial records, which was next on her list for the day. But that didn't mean she couldn't feel happy, did it?

She had just opened one of her favorite Mo Willems books—Piggie and Elephant always made her laugh—when a loud thump at the front of the store caught her attention.

Figuring someone must be trying to get her attention from outside, she got up from her cross-legged position on the floor. But as she headed for the door, she didn't see anyone standing on the pavement.

That was when she realized a massive stack of mail had been pushed through the brass mail slot. There hadn't been any letters or bills waiting for her when she'd arrived two days ago, but she supposed the island was small enough that the post office might have been holding Charlie's mail until they knew someone would be there to pick it up.

Clearly, word had spread that she was here. Though Owen had said he'd put in a good word for her with the island's residents, she also hoped to make a positive impression on her own merits.

But as Mari picked up the stack of mail, all thought of making impressions—good or otherwise—fled at the sight of the red stripes across nearly all of the envelopes.

She'd started the day hoping to find another unexpected treasure. Well, she'd found something unexpected, all right. Only it wasn't something wonderful. Just the opposite, she thought, as she thumbed through nearly a dozen past-due bills.

The solicitors had told Mari they'd paid all outstanding bills from the funds remaining in Charlie's bank account. Clearly, these had slipped through the cracks.

Mentally girding herself, she opened each envelope. A delivery of books from an estate in Wales: £2,320. A new water heater and pump: £5,642. Herbal pills sent from Japan: £976. Several hundred pounds for this month's water, electric, and gas bills.

This morning, when Mari had awakened to the sun shining and the birds singing, and Owen's kisses from last night still tingling on her lips, she had begun to believe things might not be so hard after all. That from here on out, her life would be on a steady upswing, with no bumps in the road. She'd let a couple of great kisses and some baby clothes lull her into a false sense of calm.

Now, she laid the bills on the counter where Mars had been sleeping. They easily made a pile big enough to qualify as a bump in her road. Paying the bills would not only take all of the money left in Charlie's account after probate, she would also need to draw from her own savings. And these were only the bills she'd received today. What if there were twice as many still to come?

Suddenly, the bookstore that had felt so warm and welcoming with the sun streaming through the windows felt unbearably hot and stuffy. She needed to get out of here. Needed to get away and try to clear her head. Needed to try to find the bright side of things again.

She ran upstairs, grabbed a jacket and her bag, then hurried back down and out the door onto the pavement. She was just locking up when Owen sent her a text: *Everything going okay today?*

He was so sweet to check in with her. She didn't want to lie to him. At the same time, it didn't feel fair to drop the shrapnel in his lap within mere seconds of the bomb going off. Not when she had a feeling he'd likely drop whatever important thing he was doing at work to figure out how to help her with the bill situation.

Mari had never been helpless and didn't like the idea of starting now. As an accountant, she'd been known for her resourcefulness and resilience no matter what clients threw her way. Now she just needed to put the same skills into practice in her own life.

Her fingers hovered over the keypad on her phone as she worked out how to reply. Finally, she typed: *Making good headway with the books in the children's section.*

It was, thankfully, completely true, regardless of the past-due bills that had just dropped into her life.

He sent back a thumbs-up, and the emoji made her smile. Owen always found a way to lift her out of her worries.

Standing on the sidewalk, she decided this afternoon was the perfect time to do a little exploring. Not only so that she could add data to her should-I-stay-or-should-I-go spreadsheet—but because she'd been curious about Elderflower Island for years.

The outdoor seating at the pub was nearly full, but she didn't want to sit down for a meal anyway. Instead, she would grab something from the café just up the lane. She stopped to admire a beautiful painting of the Thames hanging in the window of the art gallery next to the pub. The colors were bright, the brushstrokes bold. She could so clearly see it hanging on the living room wall in the flat, the perfect way to add some vibrancy to the dark tweeds and plaids Charlie had favored.

It was the first time she'd thought about making the space her own. It was a slightly scary thought—particularly when she was nowhere near certain, from a fiscal perspective, that she could keep the store and flat. And yet even that hint of fear couldn't stop her from noticing the beautiful hand-thrown pottery in the next window. The blues and greens reminded her of the trees and sky here. She would love to eat her breakfast porridge out of one of these unique bowls, rather than something made in a factory thousands of miles away.

She walked past the charity shop, which was next to the Elderflower Café. Walking into the café, she was enveloped by the most wonderful smells. Her stomach growled as she got in line. By the time she got to the front, she still hadn't decided what to have, it all looked so good.

"Hi," she said. "I'm new here. What do you recommend?"

The man behind the counter had a bushy beard and a cheerful face. "Everything, of course," he said with a wink. "Are you in the mood for sweet or savory?"

She didn't have to think long. "Both."

"That's what I was hoping you would say. How about I'll give you something for lunch *and* dessert?"

"Sounds perfect. And please, surprise me."

He looked approving. "I like a customer who's willing to take risks."

Ah, yes, *risks*. That was practically her middle name at this point.

"I'm Jacob, and I own the café. You look familiar, but I don't think we've met before, have we?"

"I'm Mari." She might as well tell him who she was. After all, if she did stay, they were going to be fellow island store owners. Perhaps there was even the equivalent of a Chamber of Commerce. "I'm—"

"Charlie's daughter! You have his eyes." He reached over the counter and grabbed her hand, shaking it heartily. "It is such a *pleasure* to meet you."

"Thank you. It's nice to meet you too." And it was also nice to know that the eyes she'd looked at in the mirror all these years were similar to her father's.

"Lunch is on the house," Jacob said as he handed her the meal he'd put in a to-go container.

"That's so nice of you, but I couldn't—"

"I insist. We all miss dear Charlie so much. Learning that he has a daughter to continue his brilliant legacy is so heartening."

Brilliant legacy? Mari couldn't imagine what her mother's reaction would be to that. Utter incredulity, most likely.

During their conversation, the line had grown long enough to extend out the door. "We're in the middle of our lunch rush now," Jacob said, "but I hope we can get to know each other better soon. In fact, a group of us paddle board down the Thames on Friday evenings. Why don't you join us tonight?"

"It sounds like fun, but I've got to admit that I've never paddle boarded before."

He waved that away. "It's easy. You just get on and float. My partner, Bernard, is going to be so thrilled to meet you. He absolutely loved Charlie."

"Thanks for the invitation." The woman in line behind her cleared her throat, so Mari picked up her lunch and stepped away from the counter. "I'll see you on the river tonight. And thank you, again, for lunch."

Back outside, she walked past the old concert hall. Even in its current dilapidated state, she could get a sense of what it must have been like in the sixties and seventies, with its grand staircase and large marquee. The café, the gallery, the boutiques all looked so current, so fashionable and bustling. Alice had said she hoped one of her brothers would take the concert hall project on. Given how much work it seemed Mari was going to have to put in to resuscitate the bookstore, she tipped an imaginary hat to him for even considering it.

Across the way, the gates to the manor house and grounds were open. The enormous home seemed slightly spooky and had an unlived-in look about it, but the garden was full of people walking dogs, pushing strollers, kicking soccer balls, and eating lunch on the lawn.

At an unoccupied bench on one of the side paths, Mari sat down to unwrap her meal. The personal-sized bacon and spinach quiche, rainbow side salad of shredded vegetables in a delicious vinaigrette, and a Bakewell tart for dessert made her realize again just how hungry she was. What's more, she had loved everything she'd eaten in England.

From her research over the years, she'd read more than one article about how Britain had transformed its lackluster culinary reputation into that of a global leader on the food front. Though everything she'd eaten so far had been simply put together, whether scones and jam, Chinese food, or this café lunch, it was all fresh and made with obvious care.

She enjoyed people-watching while she ate, and once she finished, she headed off to explore the trails on the manor's extensive property. An hour later, lost in a copse of trees, she asked one of the dog walkers to point her back toward the entrance gates.

Her feet were sore by the time she made it back to Elderflower Lane, but it was a good kind of ache. She could easily see herself doing this every day—stopping in at the café for her lunch, then going for a stroll in the park. It was so different from her life in Santa Monica, where she'd eaten lunch at her desk, going out only if they were hosting a client. She worked out in a gym along with everyone else she knew, not because the weather in Southern California wasn't great for exercising outside, but because parking at the local trails was a madhouse.

While she'd walked today, rather than trying to work out how to deal with her father's bills, she'd simply appreciated the beautiful landscape. Since she was still full of energy, rather than heading back to the bookstore to get back to work, Mari continued her explorations. For the next hour or so, she meandered down winding lanes of cute cottages. She loved the brightly colored doors, the shiny brass and silver knockers in an array of shapes, the red post boxes, the cobblestone- and brick-lined streets, the herb gardens in small plots.

One section of connected cottages had been turned into artists' studios, and she longed to peek inside at what the painters or sculptors or woodworkers were making. She had never been great with her hands—even knitting tripped her up—but that didn't stop her from appreciating the talents of others. She would love to support local artists—perhaps by displaying a revolving selection of their paintings and other creations in the bookstore.

She tucked the idea away for later use. All her budding ideas and plans hinged on whether she could figure out how to get the store into the black *and* if she decided to stay.

At last, she rounded the corner to the Elderflower Island Rowing Club and Boatyard. Stretching a city block, the yard had several fishing boats up on stands on the far side of the building, a rental area where people could take rowboats and kayaks out for the day, sculls of every size stacked on metal racks, and a section devoted to paddle boards.

The building was a blur of activity, with men and women of all ages either working on boats, bringing watercraft back in, or getting ready to take something out on the river.

"Mari, you came!"

She turned to see Jacob approaching, hand in hand with the man she assumed must be his partner. How had the entire afternoon slipped by so quickly? Fortunately, she was dressed in the same leggings, tennis shoes, and windbreaker as everyone who was grabbing boards and paddles off the rack.

"Mari, this is Bernard. Bernard, this is Charlie's daughter. She's here to take over the bookshop."

Bernard surprised her by throwing his arms around her. "I'm so happy you've come to us from America." He put his hands on her shoulders and scanned her face. "I could have seen the resemblance from a mile away. You're the spitting image of him—if he had been a beautiful woman, of course."

Her mom hadn't kept any pictures of Charlie, apart from one of their wedding day that Mari had found buried in a dusty box in the attic. It was faded enough that Mari had never really had a good picture of her father inside her head. And now she was learning that she'd had a clear picture of him all along, simply by looking in the mirror. Not only was Mari fair, without so much as a hint of her mother's olive skin, but everything from the shape of her eyes to the texture of her hair differed from her mother's. Because she looked so much like Charlie.

"Let's get you outfitted for the paddle board." Bernard tugged her into the boathouse, while Jacob held up life vests in a variety of sizes to see which would fit best.

★ ★ ★

Owen had dutifully stayed at his desk, working through business matters, since eight o'clock that morning. All the while, however, he'd been thinking about Mari.

As he'd said to her last night, he didn't want to make the mistake of coming on too strong. Especially when she already had more than enough on her plate. But he hadn't been able to resist sending her a text earlier to see how she was doing. Though he was relieved to hear that things were going well today, he was a tad disappointed that he didn't have a good excuse to drop by during the workday.

At a quarter past five, when his grandmother called his name from her desk at the front window, he was more than happy to close his laptop and step away from email.

"How's it going, Gran?"

"I'm having trouble with the big reveal. The villain just decided to turn into a good guy, so needless to say, it isn't going well." His grandmother pointed out the window to the boathouse along the water's edge. "Your paddle board group is gathering. I'm sure they're all wondering where you've been."

One of the things Owen loved most about living in London was easy access to the water. He'd grown up sailing in it and as a member of the rowing club. This past year, however, he hadn't felt comfortable being so far out of reach, in case his grandmother needed him. It would be impossible to make his way back up the river quickly on a board or kayak if she had another stroke. In lieu of getting out on the river, he'd taken to running miles every day on a treadmill in the back cottage and worked out with free weights.

"We saw Jacob and Bernard at the pub last week," he reminded her.

"Go and be with your friends. I won't take no for an answer."

It was one thing for his grandmother to encourage him to spend time with Mari. He put that down to romantic intent. But what was all this about? Anything out of the ordinary worried him. He wasn't going to miss a crucial sign again.

"I can go another time."

Mathilda shot him a look. "What part of my last sentence confused you? 'Yes, Gran' will suffice."

He rarely saw her act this way—imperious and commanding. Her color looked good, though, and her words were crisp. Maybe having trouble with her chapter had made her grumpy, and a little space would be a good thing for her. For both of them, if he was being completely honest.

"Yes, Gran." He gave her a kiss on the cheek, then grabbed a cap and jacket from the rack near her front door as he headed out.

The air smelled sweet, and the sun was a glowing ball in the sky as it began its slow descent. Oliver and Jill, who managed the boathouse, looked pleased to see him. "Welcome back, Owen!"

He headed into the boathouse to get his board and paddle…and walked into Mari. Literally.

CHAPTER TWELVE

"Owen?" Mari was wearing a lifejacket over her sweatshirt. Her free hand rested on his chest as she'd steadied herself, and he held her at the waist, though she was no longer in danger of wobbling over. Her cheeks were flushed as she looked up at him, her eyes bright. And all he could think about was dipping his head to kiss her. "I didn't know you were going to be here."

"Gran kicked me out."

And now he knew why. His grandmother must have seen Mari go into the boathouse with Jacob and Bernard. Though Mathilda had been in bed by the time he returned from the bookshop last night, and they hadn't discussed Mari again today, so she couldn't possibly know about their kiss, his grandmother obviously hadn't forgotten her intention to get them together.

As the oldest of five, Owen was far more used to telling people what to do than obeying orders. But when it came to Gran scheming to set him and Mari up, Owen wasn't about to complain.

"Our fearless leader has returned!" As soon as Mari stepped out of Owen's arms, Bernard gave him a bear hug. "Your gran looked great at the pub last weekend. We were hoping you'd find your way back to us sooner rather than later, weren't we, Jacob?"

His partner nodded. "Good to see you back in the boathouse, Owen. And it seems you already know Mari."

Her cheeks were still flushed as she explained, "Owen has been helping me sort out Charlie's things in the bookstore." She shook her head. "I mean *bookshop*. I keep forgetting that's how you say it in England."

"Call it whatever you want—store, shop, hub, joint," Bernard said. "As long as you're planning to reopen it."

Though she smiled in response, Owen could see that she also felt a little put on the spot. "I'm still trying to get my head above water," she said with a laugh, obviously trying to downplay the massive cleanup job ahead of her in the bookstore.

"Stop pressuring her," Jacob said to Bernard. Then he turned to Owen. "We were just about to give Mari the basics on how to use her paddle, but I think it would be better if I got this one out on the river before he puts his foot any further into his mouth."

With that, Jacob pulled Bernard away, leaving Owen and Mari alone.

"They mean well," he said softly. "No one wants to pressure you into doing something you're not comfortable with."

"Both Jacob and Bernard are absolutely lovely, and I know they wouldn't want to pressure me. I just hate the thought of letting anyone down," she confessed.

"You won't." When she didn't look convinced, he decided to give her some room to breathe by changing the subject. "Have you spent much time on a paddle board?"

She shook her head. "I always meant to try it, but somehow I never seemed to find the time. Jacob and Bernard are remarkably persuasive, though. I'd like to stay out of the river, if at all possible, so I'll happily take any pointers you've got."

"Once you get your balance, it's a piece of cake, especially when the water is like glass." He showed her where to stand on the board, how far apart to set her feet, and where to grip the paddle. "In a pinch, you can always lower yourself to a kneeling or seated position, which will further stabilize you." When she still looked a little uncertain, he said, "I'll be beside you the whole way, Mari. I won't let anything happen to you."

She met his eyes, staring at him for a long moment. Finally, she smiled. "I know you won't." Then she picked up her board to carry it to the river's edge.

"Ready?"

He smiled back, never happier about his grandmother's meddling. "Ready."

Some people wobbled around the first time they got on a paddle board before finding their boarding legs. Others fell into the water. But Mari picked it up right away.

The tide was slack, perfect for paddle boarding. And the water was calm enough that they barely had to push their paddles into the water to glide across the surface.

She silently concentrated on her strokes until she'd gained the confidence to multitask by talking at the same time. "How long has it been since you've come out with the group?"

"A year. Ever since my grandmother had a stroke."

She looked upset by the information. "Oh no! I had no idea."

"Which is exactly how she wanted it. We canceled her appearances, claiming she needed more time to write, and asked everyone who knew the truth to keep the news to themselves. She already hated how much writing time she'd lost while recovering. The last thing she wanted was for people to question the quality of her new books, or suggest that the stroke had stolen any of her creativity."

"On the contrary," Mari said, "now that I know

about it, all I can think is how marvelous her dedication to her writing must be. Instead of letting a stroke stop her in her tracks, I bet her books will be even richer now for the experience."

If Owen hadn't already liked Mari so much, her boundless confidence in Mathilda's talent and commitment to her writing would have done it. "It's what I've been telling her, but she refuses to listen."

"She sounds delightfully stubborn," Mari said with a smile.

He laughed. "It's hard to believe you haven't met her yet. She would have come to the shop to greet you, but she wanted to give you a little time to settle in first."

"I'd love to meet her. And I can come to her, if that's easier, depending on how her recovery has gone."

"She's doing really well. There are likely some faculties that she'll never regain use of one hundred percent, but the slowdowns in her speech and gait only tend to surface when she's tired. I moved into her back cottage to help out." Before she could make the mistake of painting him as some kind of hero, he explained, "Of everyone in the family, it made the most sense for me to look after her. I'm already there during the day, so staying into the evenings wasn't a big deal."

"It's really lovely how you watch out for her."

His gut clenched. As open as she'd been with him, it suddenly didn't feel right not to be just as open with her. "There's more to the story." Owen had never fallen off his board, but just then he caught the edge of his paddle on the water in such a way that he nearly catapulted himself in. "It was my fault."

She frowned. "How could your grandmother having a stroke be *your* fault?"

"Not the stroke, but the severity of it. If I had been in the cottage, if I had seen her fall and called the ambulance immediately, there would have been less damage, and her recovery would have been much easier."

"Of course I understand that you wish you had been there to call for help at the first signs. But I can't imagine your job entails sitting at your grandmother's side twenty-four seven—or that she would want you to do that."

"You're right. She has never asked more of me than she would any other business manager. But the stroke happened during the middle of the workday, when I was away at a meeting. One I went to behind her back." He made himself look Mari in the eye as he admitted, "A major streaming service offered me a job heading up their literary licensing division. I was flattered and couldn't resist an afternoon of seeing how badly they wanted me. When I got back from the city that night, Gran was lying on the floor, barely conscious."

"I'm so sorry, Owen."

So was he. "You're the only one who knows the full story."

"Thank you for telling me," she said softly. "I promise to keep your confidence. But does your grandmother know you feel this way? That you haven't stopped blaming yourself for not being there for her?"

He shook his head. "I've never wanted to admit how close I came to betraying her."

"But what if you did talk with her about what happened that day?" Mari asked. "Do you really believe that's how she would look at it? As a betrayal? Or would she understand that you're only human? I'm sure she's messed up before, just like each and every one of us has. But you wouldn't want her to beat herself up for her mistakes forever, would you?"

Mari's questions stopped him as though he'd run aground. He'd been too riddled with guilt to think about the situation from any other perspective. "Gran isn't the kind of person who holds a grudge."

"Then why are you holding one against yourself?" When he didn't immediately reply, she added, "I can't help but think that if you told her what you just told me, both of you would feel so much better."

Owen had thought Mari needed his help. But maybe he needed *her* help just as much.

"I'll sit down with her tonight and lay it all out."

Mari gave him an encouraging smile. "I'm sure you'll feel a million times better once you get everything off your chest."

"Maybe. Or maybe not. But you're right that, either way, I need to be honest with her." And he wasn't sure he would ever have seen it without Mari's help. "Thank you for listening—and for showing me a fresh perspective on the situation."

"Anytime," she said, giving him another smile. A smile that made him desperate to kiss her again. So desperate that if he wasn't positive they'd both end up in the river, he would have leaned over on his board to taste her lips right there and then.

She bit her lip, looking as though she was trying to make a decision about something. The rest of the group paddled back around toward the boathouse, and she remained silent while they did the same. It wasn't until they were pointing upriver again that she spoke.

"I could use a fresh perspective too."

"Did something happen at the shop?"

She nodded. "The postman came. I think Charlie's mail must have been held until word got out that I was here." She looked a little green, and not from motion sickness. "There were more than a half-dozen bills. Big ones."

Owen uttered a low curse. He wished Mari's situation were easier, cleaner, simpler. Though he'd offered to do Charlie's books many times over the years, her father had never taken him up on it, so Owen had no idea what kind of financial position Mari had been left in. He had a feeling it wasn't in the black.

"There's not quite enough left in his accounts after probate to pay these bills," she continued, answering his unspoken question. "I'm going to need to pull from my savings to completely cover them."

Owen had spent most of his life ironing out his younger siblings' problems. In fact, going to work for his grandmother had been an extension of that. Now, he was already working out how to solve Mari's problems—finalizing the TV contracts for Mathilda's *Bookshop on the River* series would be a good start, although it would be a while before the network lawyers signed off and wrote her a check—when it suddenly hit him that what she needed most of all wasn't a to-do list.

The best thing he could give her was a reminder of who she was at her core.

"Yesterday, when we were talking at dinner, you told me that owning a bookshop is your dream come true. I know opening those bills must have been tough. I know it might not be easy to find the money to pay them. And I know we only met a little more than two days ago. Nonetheless, I'm one hundred percent sure you deserve to live your dream—and that you're not going to let anything keep you from doing just that."

He hadn't meant to give a full-on speech, and when he couldn't read her expression for several strokes of their paddles, he worried he might have overstepped the mark.

Finally, she spoke. "I'll admit that I nearly hit the panic button when I first saw the bills. That's why I ended up walking around the island all afternoon, because I thought it might help clear my mind. And it did, but not in the way I thought. I didn't crunch any numbers. I didn't think of any brilliant guerrilla marketing moves. I simply enjoyed being here. Exploring the island I'd only ever dreamed about from afar." Her lips turned up slightly at the corners. "Charlie obviously also had a dream to run a bookstore, and he made it happen despite having lost his family because of his drinking problem." Her smile slipped a little as she said, "For as much as I loved him when I was a little girl, after the way he left, I can't honestly say that I feel like I owe it to him to save his store. It's more that I owe it to *myself*. To see if it's possible to make *my* dreams come to life." She smiled at the sound of Jacob's laughter ahead of them. "I still have a lot to assess and think over before I'm ready to commit one hundred percent to staying and trying to make the bookstore profitable, but it's a nice bonus to know how much everyone else on the island seems to want me to succeed, and to stay."

They paddled up to the shore in front of the boathouse.

"We all do, Mari." Especially him. Because from the first moment Owen had set eyes on Mari, he'd had the feeling that she was the missing key to all of his own dreams finally coming true.

CHAPTER THIRTEEN

Fifteen minutes later, they had put away their life jackets, paddles, and boards and headed across the street to his grandmother's cottage.

Once they were on the pavement, Mari put her hand over his. "Good luck with your talk tonight. But given how much you and your grandmother clearly adore each other, I very much doubt you're going to need it."

He threaded his fingers through hers, then lifted her hand to his lips. "Thank you."

He was surprised when she tugged him closer and kissed him. As soon as their mouths met, her body melted into his. It wasn't until a passing car honked that he remembered where they were—standing in Elderflower Lane, kissing in broad daylight. Still, it wasn't easy to let her go. Not when all he wanted was to pull her closer.

"I should get back to the store," she said in a voice that didn't seem quite steady. "If you need anything…you know where I am."

Hell yes, he already needed more of her kisses. But she was right that he should talk with his grandmother immediately. A year was more than long enough to have kept the truth from her.

Mathilda was waiting with a freshly brewed pot of tea when he walked in. "How was the river?"

"Like glass."

"And how was Mari?"

"Lovely as ever."

She put out a plate of biscuits, then two cups and saucers. "I was hoping you would invite her in."

"She'd very much like to meet you. But tonight, I'd appreciate the chance to speak with you privately."

One brow rose as she poured the tea. "From your tone, this doesn't sound like it's going to be about business. Is it?"

"No." He ran a hand over his face. "Well, not entirely."

She sat, then gestured for him to continue.

"Over the past few years, several companies have tried to recruit me."

"As well they should. You're the best of the best." It twisted his gut tighter to see the loving pride on her face.

"Thank you for saying that, Gran. Although you might reconsider by the time I've told you the whole truth."

"Whatever it is you have to say, you'll always be the grandson I love and the colleague I respect." She took a sip of her tea. "Now, out with it."

"Before I say anything more, I want you to know that I never truly planned to leave you, Gran. However..." He blew out a harsh breath. "I wasn't immune to flattery."

"No one is, darling."

"The day you had your stroke, I told you I'd gone to Notting Hill to meet with a book binder to discuss special hardcover editions. I did meet with him, Gran, but afterward, I was wined and dined by a major streaming service that wanted to bring me on board to head up their TV licensing division." They'd ordered oysters that day for lunch. He hadn't been able to eat one since. "While you were lying on the floor, desperate for help, I was getting drunk on champagne and pretty words about how great they thought I was." Champagne was at the very bottom of his drinks list now too. "I can't tell you how much I wish I could do that day over again."

"Have you finished beating yourself up?"

"Honestly? I don't know that I ever will. How can I stop blaming myself for not being here for you when you needed me most?"

"You just do." She made it sound so easy, so final. "First, by knowing that I don't blame you for anything."

"Why wouldn't you, when I went behind your back at the worst possible time?"

"Of course I wish you had been honest with me, Owen, but I understand why you weren't. We both know that family working together isn't without complications. Sometimes we don't see eye to eye. Sometimes you want to stretch your wings in one direction, while I want to fly in another. But throughout the ups and the downs of our entwined careers, we always love each other. And though we may spend plenty of hours together looking at book sales figures, or copyeditors' changes, or a whole host of other business concerns, our love for one another is, at both the beginning and the end of each day, the only thing that truly matters."

"Always, Gran. You know I'd do anything for you."

"And you have." She reached for his hand. "I know how many job offers you've turned down to stay with me—offers you would be crazy not to listen to. Offers I suspect you're even crazier to have rejected. Besides, I'm just as driven by ego as anyone." Before he could protest that she didn't have an egotistical bone in her body, she said, "Every day that you're still here with me, working your magic on my behalf, when a dozen bigger and brighter worlds could be your oyster, I'm selfishly pleased. So you see, you're not the only one who owes an apology. I owe you one for holding on too tightly."

"Never too tightly, Gran."

She squeezed his hand again, then let go to pick up her teacup. "Now that we've had this much-needed heart-to-heart, and you understand that you have absolutely nothing to feel guilty for, I hope that you will no longer feel the need to spend every spare moment at my side, or be in your office around the clock."

"I promise to work on the guilt," he said, "but I don't think I'll ever be able to stop worrying about leaving you alone too long."

"I hired you to run my business, Owen, not to make sure I live forever." His grandmother had always been blunt, but never more so than tonight. "I dearly hope I don't have another stroke. But if I do?" She held his gaze. "Whatever happens to me won't be your fault, wherever you are, near or far."

Though he knew it would take a while for her words to sink in—and that a part of him would always be compelled to watch over her—he nodded. "Got it, Gran."

"Now," she said as she picked up a biscuit and crunched into it, "I'm planning to visit Mari tomorrow to say hello."

"The two of you are going to hit it off," he said.

Then he had to add, "Do you know why Charlie never spoke of her to anyone?"

"Yes, I do. I tried to talk him out of it many times over the years, but it was no use. As I said earlier, blame never helps anyone, regardless of whether it's aimed out or in. If Charlie could have forgiven himself, he could have had the chance at a relationship with his daughter." She gave her head a shake, as though to dislodge the dark mood. "Now, I don't want to keep you from dropping by the bookshop again tonight if Mari is expecting you."

It was hugely tempting to go to Mari and continue their kiss where they'd left off. But he wanted to make sure his relationship with his grandmother was completely solid. "Actually, Gran, though I know you and I could probably both use some time apart after the past year, if it's all right with you, tonight I'd quite like to spend some time thrashing you at Happy Families."

Mathilda laughed at his sneaky tie-in to her earlier statement about family coming first. "Sometimes you really are too clever for your own good."

He winked at her, and as he went into the living room to fetch the game, he sent a quick text to Mari, thanking her for pushing him to finally do the right thing by talking openly with Mathilda and letting her know that it had gone well.

When she sent him back a smiley face and then

mentioned that jet leg had returned with a vengeance, he wished her a good night's sleep. And realized, as he tucked his phone into his pocket, that already he couldn't imagine his life without her in it.

CHAPTER FOURTEEN

Mari woke at first light, nearly ten hours after she'd gone to bed. She couldn't believe how hard jet lag had hit her half a week into her time in England, though Carson had warned her that it was normal for her body clock to swing back and forth as it settled into a new time zone. Her multi-hour stroll around the island, followed by paddle boarding, must have kicked her exhaustion into overdrive. Not to mention her concern on Owen's behalf while she waited to hear how his talk had gone with his grandmother. She'd been so relieved to get his text confirmation that all was well.

The thing was, even as she'd told Owen that coming clean with his grandmother would surely lift the weight from his shoulders, she'd recognized her own hypocrisy. All these years, Mari had deliberately kept her secret fascination with Elderflower Island from her parents. Now that she was here, and it was even more wonderful than she'd anticipated, she knew she couldn't keep it secret for much longer.

And as she stood at the bedroom window looking

out at the still deserted street below, she could no longer deny the truth: She never should have kept her dreams a secret. Choosing to play it safe by keeping her true desires quiet for so long was only going to make things worse now. Her mother would surely feel blindsided by the news that Mari was seriously considering turning her dreams of living in England into reality.

The easier choice would be to continue telling herself that she wanted to have all the answers before she sat Donna down for a big, potentially life-changing conversation. It was what she'd said to her mom on the phone, after all, that she needed time to think things through. But Mari knew that was just more of the same avoidance she'd been practicing her whole life. She'd vowed not to do it again. And she'd meant it.

She walked barefoot out of the flat and into the store to let out Mars. Then she went back upstairs, flicked on the kettle, and brought her laptop over to the kitchen table. Her mother would be asleep in California, but if Mari sent an email now, it would be waiting in Donna's inbox when she woke up.

Mari logged into her email, opened a new message window, and didn't let herself overthink as she typed:

Mom,

Hello from Elderflower Island! I know I said I needed some time to think, but I really do want to speak with you about things as soon as you get this email. Life in England has been an adventure so far. I got a chance to explore the island a bit yesterday. I even went out on a paddle board on the Thames with some new friends!

I'm looking forward to filling you in on all the exciting developments. I'll look forward to getting your call.

Love,
Mari

She hit *send* before she could change her mind, given that it was unlikely her mother would be pleased to hear of the *exciting developments* in Mari's life since arriving in London.

Before she closed her computer, she wrote one more email.

Carson,

I'd say I hope you're not working too hard, but I know you are. One day soon, I'd love for you to come to Elderflower Island for some rest and relaxation. You'd love walking the trails and rowing the river. And, of course, you'd have a fantastic flat to stay in while you're here.

If you're wondering if you read that paragraph right, you have. Despite some less than great news about Charlie's finances, I'm seriously considering trying to make bookstore ownership work. I don't know yet if the numbers will add up so that I can actually pull it off, but I can't help wanting to try. You're probably laughing as you read this, because you always *knew what I wanted, didn't you?*

Big hugs from London,
Mari

After sending the email, she closed her laptop, then made a pot of tea and spread lemon curd over a scone. From the kitchen table, she could see the river coming to life outside the window. Though the sun had risen only fifteen minutes earlier, there were already a good half-dozen people on the water in sculls and kayaks. The street was still mostly empty, but there were people biking and running along the riverfront path in Twickenham and St. Margarets. The birds were also out in full force, flying from tree to tree, periodically diving down to capture worms from the shoreline.

She could never look at this view and take it for granted. The coast of California was stunning, but it had never moved her the way this quintessentially British setting did.

All the more reason to solve the issue of more unexpected bills. She could cover them with her personal savings, but as an accountant, she knew keeping that money as a cushion would be better. Perhaps Charlie had a stash of money she hadn't yet found?

If there was any chance of that, she needed to go through the rest of Charlie's things.

Yes, she still had to clean up the rest of the bookstore. But that could wait a little longer while she looked inside the antique chest in the corner of the living room and the boxes in the back of his closet.

Purposefully, she walked into the living room and moved the hand-thrown bowl from the top of the old wooden chest. It was such an imposing piece of furniture that she would have instinctively used it to store things that were important to her. But the last thing she expected to see upon opening the heavy lid was a stash of file folders. It was the strangest filing cabinet she'd ever come across.

Somehow, though, this fit the Charlie she was coming to know to a T.

Pulling out the dozen folders, she thumbed through the papers inside. The good news was that they contained local and national company licenses, which would certainly be helpful to have on hand. Unfortunately, there was no buried treasure beyond that. Certainly no stash of cash to pay off his bills.

Okay, then, she'd have to look in the beaten-up boxes in the back of his closet. Though it seemed an unoriginal hiding place, it still couldn't be overlooked.

Despite having already spent an evening with Owen clearing Charlie's things, it wasn't easy to go back into his room. Though she had only faint memories of her father, the scent of his cologne from the bottle on his dresser—a brand she now knew was called Green Irish Tweed—was one that immediately made her think of him.

Mari pulled the two cardboard boxes out of the closet and set them on the bed. Lifting the cover of one, she was surprised to find several smaller boxes inside.

What had she just discovered?

Carefully, Mari opened the biggest box. Inside was a porcelain doll, wearing a pretty outfit complete with hat, gloves, and shoes, almost exactly like the one she'd gotten for her fourth birthday.

In another box was UNO, one of her favorite card games. She'd started playing it when she was five.

The next box held Twister, which she and Carson had played endlessly when she was six.

One after the other, she laid the contents of the boxes on top of the bed. Each item was exactly what she would have wanted for her seventh birthday, or her tenth, or her thirteenth, or her eighteenth. All the way down to the final gift: a signed copy of one of her favorite stories, *The Book Thief* by Markus Zusak.

Her father hadn't seen her since she was three…and yet, from all these birthday presents that he'd never sent her, he'd still known her so well.

Grief at all the time they'd lost—not only the birthdays they hadn't celebrated together, but also the normal, day-to-day moments—warred with another bloom of hope inside her chest.

Yesterday's bills had been a blow. But though nothing inside these boxes would help pay them, they were exactly what she'd needed to find to give her another much-needed boost.

She still didn't understand why he'd stayed away, but at least she was beginning to see a path to forgiveness.

★ ★ ★

After making her big discoveries, Mari decided to take a little breather by burying her head in the History section in the bookstore. The hours flew by as she transformed it into an enticing area for history buffs to browse for hours on end.

It wasn't until her stomach let out a massive grumble that she realized it was two hours past noon. She should really find something to eat soon, perhaps even popping into the pub across the street. But just as she was about to head up to the flat to grab her purse, she noticed that a side table with a red wool throw over it was actually a small file cabinet. She had overlooked it several times already. Only the fact that the throw was slightly askew and showing a full metal base had made her wonder what kind of table could be beneath the cloth.

Mari had given up hope of finding a filing cabinet anywhere in her father's place of business. On the one hand, she could appreciate all he'd managed to accomplish with his easygoing business management style. Not only was the store clearly well respected and well loved, it had also been in business for twenty-five years. On the other hand, one of the reasons Mari enjoyed her work at her stepfather's accounting firm was because she was innately organized. She loved lists—making them, and checking things off them. She also appreciated order. Making a plan could be nearly as much fun as executing it. Tonight, once she'd exhausted her search of the store and flat, she would sit down and start making a point-by-point business, marketing and promotion plan to reopen the store.

It hadn't escaped her that the only people to come by since she'd arrived had been Owen, Alice, and the mail carrier—there was not a customer in sight. Once she'd paid off the bills and assessed her finances, she would list each and every thing she could do to get the word out that the bookstore was open for business, with word-of-mouth, social media sharing, and other inexpensive marketing methods at the top of her list.

The wool throw was dusty, and she sneezed as she

took it off. She carried it out the back door to a narrow cobblestone alley and snapped the blanket in the air several times to shake off the dust.

A few fluffy clouds moved slowly overhead in the bright blue sky. Birds sang as they flew between treetops. And yet, when she breathed in deep, she could smell a hint of coming rain. Everyone in Southern California believed they had the best weather, that blindingly bright sun was all it took to be happy—but Mari would take London weather any day of the week. True, she hadn't experienced a rainstorm or impenetrable fog yet, but she had a feeling she was going to enjoy them both.

When she was satisfied that the throw was dust-free, she folded it up and went back inside. With the blanket on a nearby chair, she opened the top drawer of the filing cabinet. But instead of holding files, it was stuffed full of black hardcover notebooks. The kind artists drew in.

Curious, Mari lifted one out and opened it.

On the first page was a drawing of a little girl holding hands with her father. They were walking in a grove of chestnut trees. At the top of the page, in dark lettering, were the words *Playing Conkers with Mars*.

Even if she hadn't seen her nickname, she couldn't deny that the little girl looked remarkably like her as a young child. And the man had to be Charlie.

Mari's hands shook as she turned the page and realized the drawing on the first page had been intended as book cover art. Within the journal was a beautifully illustrated and written children's story about a man and his daughter collecting conkers to play a game together.

She'd been looking for buried treasure.

What she'd found was beyond her wildest imagination.

She was only halfway through the first journal—how many stories had Charlie written, and were they all about the two of them?—when her phone buzzed. Still stunned beyond belief by what she'd just read, she pulled it out of her pocket on autopilot.

Her mother's name and face were on the screen. Even though Mari had emailed to ask Donna to call as soon as she woke up, Mari knew she couldn't talk to her now. Hours ago, when she'd been sitting at her laptop sending the note, she hadn't known the truth of just how deep Charlie's love for her had gone. Now that she did, how could she possibly have a rational conversation with her mother when she hadn't yet processed this latest revelation herself?

A knock at the front door gave Mari the excuse she needed to put the phone back in her pocket without answering it. And when she got close enough to the door to see through the window, though she had never met the person standing outside, she recognized her immediately.

Mathilda Westcott.

Mari's heart beat even faster as she unlocked the door. "Hello." She felt her lips wobble as she tried to smile at Owen's grandmother. The other woman hadn't yet had a chance to speak when Mari held up the book. Mathilda was one of the only people who might understand just how big a deal this was, given what Owen had said about how close Charlie and Mathilda had been. "I found this. Charlie wrote a children's book. About the two of us. There is a whole stack of these stories."

Mathilda came in and closed the door behind her. "May I see it?"

Mari handed her the notebook. The older woman's hands were far steadier than hers as she opened it carefully.

Mathilda had read only a few pages when she closed the cover, gave it back to Mari, and opened her arms wide. Mari didn't think twice before walking into them.

"My darling Marina." Owen's grandmother held on tight and didn't let go for a long while.

Not that Mari wanted to pull away. She desperately needed someone to talk to about Charlie's journals—but more than that, it was as though Mathilda

Westcott had known this and magically appeared right when Mari needed her most.

Almost as though Charlie had sent her himself...

"Why don't you come back to the cottage with me? I'll text Owen and ask him to have a pot of tea waiting for us. And then when you're ready, we can finally get to know one another."

Mari couldn't think of anything she'd rather do right now than drink a cup of steaming tea in a cozy cottage with Owen and Mathilda as she tried to make sense of the way everything in her life had turned upside down since arriving on Elderflower Island.

CHAPTER FIFTEEN

All day, Owen had been tethered to his telephone. The conference calls with the producers in France that he'd put off earlier in the week could no longer be ignored. But as they hammered out details and timelines, he'd been thinking of Mari.

His grandmother had left fifteen minutes ago for the bookshop. He'd wanted to accompany her, but that was right when the president of the French network joined the call. Planning to follow as soon as he could, he had gestured for her to go without him.

His grandmother's text made his chest tighten with concern: *Bringing Mari home for tea after a huge shock. Please put the kettle on.*

Though the network president didn't seem ready to wrap up the call just yet, Owen made his excuses, then left his desk without giving work another thought. For the past year, he'd lived and breathed business. At last, he could see how far overboard he'd gone. Yes, his work on behalf of his grandmother's books was important, but it should never have become the be-all and end-all of his life. There was no question that last night's talk with Mathilda had helped absolve him of a great deal of the guilt he'd been carrying around for the past year. But what felt just as momentous was that he hadn't been able to shake Mari from his thoughts since the moment they'd met.

He didn't want to shake her away. Just the opposite, in fact.

He wanted nothing more than the chance to know Mari better. And not only because of their spectacular kisses...although he wouldn't deny just how many times he'd replayed them in his head.

As he made tea, he tried to figure out what the latest shock could be after yesterday's nasty pile-of-bills surprise. Owen loved Charlie—they all had. And he dearly wished Mari's father had still been here today. But that didn't mean he could ignore the man's faults, especially where his daughter was concerned.

On top of being absent for nearly Mari's entire life, Charlie had left her with a filthy flat, a run-down bookshop, and a stack of unpaid bills. Owen knew his perspective on families was different from many others'. His parents had been happily married for more than three decades, and he was close to his four siblings. But was it too much to ask for parents to openly love their children without making them feel as though they'd done something wrong at some point along the way?

The kettle was whistling by the time he heard the front door open. He poured water into the pot and brought it over to the table just as Mari and Mathilda came into the kitchen.

Mari's face was pale, and she was clutching a stack of black art journals.

"Thank you for making tea, darling." His grandmother led Mari over to a chair and sat her down, then moved to the cupboard to get out her stash of chocolate Hobnobs, her special biscuits that Owen knew not to eat, or suffer the consequences. "A biscuit and a sip of sweet tea will do wonders."

Just as his grandmother predicted, a few minutes later, the color had returned to Mari's cheeks. When she looked up, it was as though she had only just realized Owen was in the room.

"Hi."

He smiled at her, his heart feeling like it had a soft center. "Hi."

"I found these today. Right before your grandmother came to say hello." She held out one of the notebooks. "Please, open it."

Owen had thought he knew Charlie quite well after haunting his bookshop for a good twenty-five years. But not only had he never guessed that the other man had a daughter nearly Owen's age, he'd certainly never sussed out that the man was a brilliant illustrator and storyteller. The style of the illustrations was vaguely reminiscent of the Winnie-the-Pooh books, but not at all a copycat.

"This is you and Charlie. Playing conkers."

She nodded. "I had no idea he could draw. Or write. Or...that he loved me so much."

"He really did," Mathilda said.

Mari swallowed hard. "Did you know?"

"About you, yes. About these books, no." Mathilda gestured to one of the notebooks. "May I look at it again?" When Mari nodded, his grandmother picked it up and turned the pages carefully as she read. "Honestly, I'm not surprised to learn that he'd been writing children's books, nor that he was writing about you. Your father had a brilliant mind. One so full of books and other people's stories that it could sometimes be difficult to have a straightforward conversation. But no matter how far away he often seemed, I knew he was always thinking about you. Always loving you with everything he was."

Mari stared at the notebook open before her without seeming to see it. "If only I'd been able to talk with him before he passed away. I can't stop wishing for it, even though I know it can never come true."

Mathilda put her hand over Mari's. "I wish you had been able to spend time with him too. Charlie and I rarely argued. But we argued about this. About you. About his stubborn insistence that he must stay out of your life forever."

"All this time," Mari said in a low voice, "I thought he didn't love me anymore. Or that, maybe, he never loved me in the first place." She ran her fingertips lightly over a drawing of her and her father skipping down a lane that looked just like the one the cottage and the bookstore were on. "Now that I know he did love me, while it feels like the hugest relief ever, at the same time it makes me *more* confused. Why did he never come back into my life?"

"I've lived more than seventy years," Mathilda said, "and I still find that, more often than not, people's choices are a mystery. I can't claim to know the full ins and outs of Charlie's mind, but he and I had enough conversations about you that I feel comfortable telling you what he told me, at the very least."

"Please." Though it was clear that she wanted answers, Mari looked as though she was bracing for impact. Owen understood—it was exactly the way he was feeling himself, though this was her story, not his. It mattered to him a great deal because Mari mattered to him.

"No one and nothing on this earth meant more to your father than you, Mari." Mathilda's expression was earnest, empathy written across her face as she spoke.

"All he wanted was the very best for you. The biggest happiness. The most extraordinary life, both present and future." She paused a beat before saying, "Which was why he could never forgive himself for what happened the day you were found on a busy street while he lay passed out at home. Yes, your mother kicked him out, but the truth is that he was already planning to leave."

"Why would he want to do that?"

"For the same reason he never got in touch with you—because he believed your life would be immeasurably better without him in it."

"Because he was an alcoholic?" A hint of anger underscored Mari's question. "He could have gotten help for his addiction and still been my dad."

"I agree, but I'm afraid he couldn't see the forest for the trees. Not then. And not thirty years later. As I said, he and I argued about it—pretty much constantly once he was diagnosed with cancer. But he could never forgive himself for what almost befell you that day so long ago. I promise you, I tried every argument under the sun to sway him, but he was immovable in his belief that he didn't deserve to be your father." Though Mathilda looked as though she had more to say, she reached for her teacup instead, picking it up with a trembling hand.

"Whatever else you have to tell me, I want to hear

it," Mari insisted.

"You're a very strong woman," Mathilda noted. "I knew you would be." She took another bracing sip of tea. "Your father was strong too. Strong enough to give up drink. Strong enough to build a new life for himself on the island after losing everything that mattered to him in California. But he wasn't strong enough to give up the belief that coming back into your life would be akin to a bad-luck omen for you."

Mari frowned. "Are you saying he thought I would get sick or hurt if I saw him again? That he believed the only reason I'm alive and well is because he was never again a part of my life?"

"Unfortunately, yes. As he grew more and more ill, I held out hope that he would at least write you a letter to explain everything and tell you how he felt about you, or put together a formal will. But in those final weeks when he refused treatment, then locked all of us away, I knew nothing had changed. Worse, I was certain that he believed dying of cancer was his karmic payment for losing you. Still, I hoped that when the solicitors found you, you'd come. And I felt certain that once you were here, you'd see all the clues he surely couldn't help but subconsciously leave for you. Clues like these notebooks."

"Every day, I've found a new one," Mari confirmed. "The *Winnie-the-Pooh* signed first edition. Mars the cat. My baby clothes. And the birthday gifts he bought for me but never sent."

At last, Mathilda smiled. "Now, here you are. And I couldn't be happier to finally meet you. You're as delightful as I knew you would be."

"I'm so glad to meet you too. For so long, I've wondered about my father's life. About his business and the people he loved." Mari's eyes were damp as she said, "I'm glad that he was surrounded by such wonderful friends. Thank you for caring about him. For loving him. I always loved him, even from afar. I'm not going to lie, however, and say I'm not angry with him. He should have given me credit for being strong enough to handle whatever came my way instead of keeping his distance because he was afraid that he might 'curse' my life in some way."

"You have every right to be angry. Just as you should never doubt that he loved you more than anyone or anything in the world," Mathilda insisted again. "And I know, without a doubt, that everything he did came from a misguided sense of love. If he hadn't been so stubborn, he would have found so much joy in seeing what a lovely, bright, determined woman you are. I'm sorry that didn't come to pass. More sorry than I can ever express. But though you're right that we can't go back to change the past, I hope that what I've told you will help you move forward with a lighter and fuller heart."

"It will. It is." Mari gave his grandmother a small smile, but Owen could see her brain was still racing to process all she'd learned. "Ever since the call came from the solicitors, I've been grappling with what I should do. At the very least, I knew I should try to get the store up and running, so that when I looked for a buyer, the sales price would be higher for a current business. But after finding these notebooks and hearing everything you've just said?"

Mari met Owen's eyes for a brief moment before turning back to Mathilda.

"I can't leave. I don't think I was *ever* going to be able to leave, if I'm being totally honest. Not when simply coming to Elderflower Island and walking into the bookstore has felt like stumbling into a world of buried treasure." Her gaze lit as she spoke of the store full of all the books she so loved. "But now I'm not just going to *try* to get Elderflower Island Books up and running—I'm *definitely* going to make it work." Determination lay under every word she spoke. "I've never done anything like this before—I've worked the same accounting job for the past ten years. But I love books and bookstores, and I know this is where I'm meant to be. I can never make up for missing a lifetime with my father, but I can embrace his legacy. And put everything I am into making sure it continues."

Just as she'd thought might happen, one of the books in Charlie's shop *had* steered her in the right direction. She just hadn't ever thought it would be a book her father wrote—about *her*.

CHAPTER SIXTEEN

Mari and Owen walked together from Mathilda's cottage to the bookstore. At three in the afternoon, the island was bustling. Chatter and laughter rang out, and the enticing smell of fish and chips wafted over from the pub. But though Mari had eaten only Hobnobs since breakfast, she wasn't hungry. She'd been so up, then down, then surprised, then touched, all within a very short time span. She could barely make sense of her emotions at this point.

All she knew for sure was that she didn't want Owen to leave.

"Would you like to come in for more tea?" Her heart raced with anticipation at the thought of being alone with Owen again. She couldn't think of any other man to whom she'd reacted so powerfully.

"I'd love to come in." He stepped inside and closed the door.

After she made tea and they were seated on the couch in the living room, he asked, "How are you feeling? You've had a lot to take in since arriving on the island."

"Seven weeks ago, if you had told me any of this would happen, I wouldn't have believed it. Finally meeting Charlie's friends. Being handed the reins of his bookstore. Learning things about him that I've always longed to know. Finding out that he never forgot about me, that I mattered to him as much as he mattered to me. Discovering his immense talent as a writer and illustrator." She paused, holding his gaze before adding, "Meeting you."

The truth was that the emotions growing inside her for the man who had just walked her home felt like the biggest thing of all. She couldn't imagine what it would have been like to come to Elderflower Island without Owen being here. It still would have been a thrill to make so many discoveries about her father and to immerse herself in the wonders of life here—but it couldn't possibly have felt as sweet.

Owen reached for her hands. How she loved the feel of his palms sliding against hers, their fingers threading together. She'd never realized how sensitive her hands were, how sensitive every part of her was, until Owen touched her like this.

"I feel the same way." His expression was at once gentle, yet full of heat. "I've struggled with Gran's stroke, and my role in it, for so long. You woke me up, Mari. And not just when it comes to Gran. You've woken me up in *every* way."

It felt so natural, so perfectly right when they both leaned in to kiss. It was fiery. Passionate. Intense. And so incredibly sexy that all she wanted was to drag him into her bedroom and make love with him all night long.

Mom will never forgive me for this.

The thought came from Mari's subconscious with such force, and such venom, that she instinctively pulled away.

"Mari?" Owen stroked her cheek, searching her eyes. "Is something wrong?"

"No." But it was clearly a lie. "Yes." She scrunched her eyes shut. This was coming out all wrong. "Not with you. Nothing is wrong with you. You're perfect." Oh God, she was only digging a bigger hole for herself. First freaking out for what surely seemed like no reason at all, then going on and on about how *perfect* he was.

The corner of his mouth quirked up on one side. "I'm nowhere near perfect, as you well know." But then his half smile fell away. "Especially given that I have no business kissing you, no business wanting you the way I do, when I know you're already dealing with so much. I should be backing off, giving you space—"

"No." She shook her head. "I don't want space. Not from you. It's just that…" There was no good way to explain the spot she was in other than to spit it out. "I've already told you that my mother isn't particularly thrilled that I'm here. But it goes deeper than that. She never forgave my father for what happened, and when he died, she didn't want me to have anything to do with his flat or his bookstore or Elderflower Island—or even England, for that matter. Telling her that I'm planning to stay will be a massive blow." She had to take a sip of her drink to give herself the fortitude to say the rest. "But I'm afraid the biggest blow of all will be if she thinks I'm repeating history. You see, my father swept her off her feet with his charming accent and exotic British ancestry. She claims I'm the only good thing that came from their relationship. I know you're not Charlie, and that it's not fair to lump all charming Englishmen into the same bucket, but—"

"I'm your mother's worst nightmare, aren't I?"

She grimaced. "Pretty much."

He digested the information. "You're close to her, aren't you?"

She nodded. "As close as you are to your family."

He smiled. "That's got to be a point in my favor, wouldn't you say?"

"Normally, I would. But I'm afraid that you could solve world hunger, end all wars, and invent the cure for cancer, and my mother might still feel that I've betrayed her by being with you."

His expression darkened. "I would never want to come between you and your family, Mari." Then his hand found hers again. "But I don't want to let you go. Not now that I've finally found you."

She loved the way he refused to give up on her. Her chest ached with longing, and her heart skipped a beat with the knowledge that everything she felt for Owen, he felt too. And yet her loyalty to her family at home was strong enough to hold her back despite the yearning.

"I get where your mother's coming from," Owen continued. "Anyone would, given the circumstances of her breakup with Charlie. But if she could see how excited you were when you were talking with Gran about reopening the bookshop, if she could see the way your skin flushes and your eyes glow when we're together—I can't imagine she would want anything to steal away your happiness."

Owen's words stopped Mari in her tracks. Yesterday, on the river, he'd said that she helped him to see things with his grandmother in a new light. Today, he'd just done the same for her with her mom. "You're right that all she's ever wanted is for me to be happy."

Which meant that despite a lifetime of hiding both her true feelings for England *and* her longing to own a bookstore from her mother in order to protect her from future emotional meltdowns, it was long past time for Mari to pull out every last stop to make Donna see that running the bookstore, living on Elderflower Island, and especially being with Owen were the keys to her true and lasting happiness. And no matter how difficult that task might be, after all the hurdles she'd already jumped over this week, she realized that she felt up to it. Only it wasn't enough to send another email. It wasn't even enough to make a phone call.

"I'm going to ask her to come here," she told Owen. "That way, she can see how wonderful my life on Elderflower Island is, and I'll be able to talk with her, face-to-face, about any of her concerns or worries." Though her stomach twisted at the thought of Donna walking into Charlie's store, she said, "You're right that she loves me enough to travel here to meet me and to listen. And because she knows how much I love her, too. Once she meets you, she'll understand why you'd never hurt me the way Charlie hurt her, and she'll give us her blessing." Mentally, Mari was crossing every single finger. "She's *got* to."

"She *will*." He lifted her hands to his lips and pressed a light kiss to each of them. Her entire body was tingling as he said, "And until then, we'll be friends. Really good friends. Until we can be more." He brushed the pad of his thumb over her lips—miles beyond something *just friends* did but not quite a kiss.

"Even if I want to kiss you so badly right now that it's tearing me up inside."

Her breath caught in her throat. It was pure agony to have him so close and know she wouldn't be able to throw herself into his arms and kiss him yet. "That's how I feel too."

Owen continued to stare at her mouth for a lingering moment. "I should probably leave."

Before she could beg him to stay and to forget everything she'd just said about needing to iron things out with her mother first, he stood up.

"I'm not going to hug you," he announced. "If I do..."

She stood too. "I know." A hug would surely lead to kissing. Which, at this point, would lead inevitably to more. "I'll see you tomorrow."

His gaze was lingering, heated. "Yes, tomorrow."

For a long moment, she wasn't sure he would actually turn and leave. She could so easily picture him sweeping her into his arms, carrying her into the bedroom, and making love to her.

Or maybe they wouldn't make it that far. Maybe they'd simply rip each other's clothes off in the living room and have gloriously hot sex on the rug.

Yes. The rug definitely had her vote if it meant his arms around her and his mouth over hers. In fact, if he didn't make a move soon, she was—

"Everything you're thinking, everything you're wanting," he said in a low, slightly pained voice, "I'm thinking and wanting too." His gaze fell to her lips again before he tore it away. She got the sense that if he could have flown a transatlantic jet to pick up Donna Everett right this second and have her on Elderflower Island as soon as humanly possible, he would already have been gunning down the runway. "Once your mother is here, she'll see how happy you are. How happy living your dream of selling books makes you. How happy everyone is to welcome you into our community. And then everything will be fine."

She wanted to believe it as much as he did.

* * *

After he left, she stared at the closed door for thirty seconds, maybe longer. It took every ounce of self-control not to run after him. To convince him that throwing caution to the winds was the best possible decision they could make.

She knew it wasn't, though. Not when so much was at stake. The most important relationship in her life was the one she had with her mom. And while it wasn't perfect, it wasn't one she ever wanted to lose.

She didn't want to lose Owen either.

Fueled with determination—and other much warmer feelings that came straight from the center of her heart—she picked up the phone and dialed her parents' home number.

"Mari?" Her stepfather's voice came over the line. He'd obviously seen her cell number on caller ID. "I'm so glad you've called. I was just about to call you."

"Is everything okay?"

"Eleanor has been admitted to the hospital for emergency surgery." Eleanor was her mother's best friend and a surrogate aunt to Mari. "Your mother has gone to the hospital to be with her."

"Oh no. Is Eleanor going to be all right?"

"I certainly hope so," Gary replied. "Her appendix has flared up, and they're planning to take it out before it bursts. Evidently, it's a routine surgery but one that can have a somewhat difficult and painful recovery. Donna will be staying with her to cook and help her around the house until her daughter comes on Friday."

"Please let me know as soon as she's out of surgery. I'd like to send her a get-well-soon bouquet so that she knows I'm thinking of her. I hope Mom isn't feeling overwhelmed with it all?" If Mari had been in town, she would have volunteered to help as much as she could.

"You know your mother—she always puts on a good front, even if she's breaking apart inside. Which is why it's so good to hear your voice, honey, and hear you sounding so well. Lord knows your mother certainly doesn't need anything else to worry about right now."

Though Mari's heart was sinking at the realization that there was no way her mother could come to England any sooner than a week from now—and that seven days of hitting the pause button with Owen was sure to feel like an eternity—Mari made sure to keep her voice upbeat as she replied, "Things are going well. I've had a chance to meet some of the locals, and they've all been really nice."

"I'm glad to hear it. I keep reminding your mother not to worry about you. You're a bright young woman who has always had both her head and heart in the right place. I have every confidence in you. I'm looking forward to hearing all about your experiences when you get back."

It was on the tip of her tongue to explain that she had called to ask them to come to England because she *wasn't* coming back. But given that Donna was likely already worried sick about Eleanor, the last thing she needed at the moment was another reason to panic. "Thanks, Dad. I don't want to disturb Mom at the hospital, so could you let her know I called? Whenever she's able to give me a call back would be great." And hopefully by then, Donna would be better rested and more able to take in what Mari needed to say to her.

"Absolutely. She'll be delighted that you called us."

Mari wasn't at all sure about that, not once she explained her reasons for calling. "Love you, Dad."

"Love you too, honey."

She hung up the phone, letting out a big sigh. She'd known it wasn't going to be easy, and that was before she'd considered unexpected complications like her mother being out of commission with a sick friend for a week.

Seven long days before she could introduce her parents to Owen and everyone else on the island, and make absolutely sure that she had their blessing. Seven long nights of keeping her hands and mouth off him. Considering she hadn't even known him until her arrival, it shouldn't seem so impossible. But it really, *really* did.

On the plus side, it meant she now had a week to get the store in as good a shape as possible. Mari knew it wouldn't erase Donna's feelings about the store having been Charlie's, but it certainly wouldn't hurt to have the business running smoothly.

It was tempting to call Owen to ask him to cancel his evening plans and to continue sorting out the store with her. But while it would be easier to rely on Owen, or his sister, or even the cat to help make her smile, that was a cop-out.

Now that she had made the decision to stay and run the bookstore, she was also going to fight for it.

Her father, she finally realized, had been a fighter. He'd fought to stay sober. He'd fought to carve out a new life here on the island. He'd even fought for her happiness, in his own misguided way.

At last, she finally understood—her happiness wasn't up to anyone else. Not her mother. Not her brother. Not Charlie.

It was up to *her*.

And gosh darn it, she was going to be happy even if it killed her!

She laughed out loud at the thought.

But at least she was laughing, right?

CHAPTER SEVENTEEN

The next morning, after Mari was drinking her second cup of extra-strong cup of coffee to combat the sleeplessness that longing for Owen had pitched her into last night, she checked her email and found a message from her brother.

Mari,

Sorry it took me so long to reply. I saw your message just as I boarded my plane to Singapore, but then the in-flight Wi-Fi went out, and I was stuck watching bad movies while wishing I was out walking the Thames path with you instead.

It's great that you're loving Elderflower Island. And it's even better to hear that you're going to try making bookstore ownership work. You're right that I was not only hoping that was what you'd decide, I was betting on it too. Although—and I hope you don't think I'm being a pushy older brother—you should take the word try *out of the equation. You're going to make it work, Mari. I have faith in your determination and abilities. You should too.*

I'm glad you're out there in London living life to the fullest. I'm hoping to fly over to your neck of the world to see you soon.

With love from a hotel room in Singapore,
Carson

Mari smiled. Carson *was* pushy. But he was also usually right. She'd sent him her email before finding Charlie's stories and had been only partly committed to making the bookstore work at that point. Of course Carson was insightful enough to pick up on that. He would be glad to know that she'd made a firm decision to stay.

Before she could email back to give him the news, the store's buzzer rang. Heading downstairs, she saw that Owen had turned up with Alice. Mari knew she and Owen must have been thinking the same thing—that given their current kissing ban, it would be easier for the time being if they weren't alone with each other. Which was why, when Jacob had dropped by fifteen minutes ago saying that he had a few hours off and wanted to see if she could use a hand in the store, she'd gratefully pulled him inside. At present, he was eating one of the scones she'd baked last night.

Mari tended to bake when her brain was working overtime to figure out the solution to a problem. Last night, between bouts of bookshelf cleaning and sorting, she'd baked scones, lemon bars, red velvet cupcakes, and chocolate chip cookies. Mars the cat had even come up to the flat to keep her company while she measured and whisked.

She'd all but cleared the shelves of the corner grocery. The owner, a man named Arjun, couldn't have been nicer. On her third visit to his store in three hours, he'd jokingly asked her if she was planning to enter *The Great British Bake Off*.

It had felt good to laugh, to be reminded that things were by no means doom and gloom. After all, she was on Elderflower Island with the entire contents of a bookstore at her fingertips, and everyone she'd met had been absolutely lovely.

Especially the man smiling at her on the sidewalk outside her store.

"Good morning, Mari." Owen leaned forward to kiss her cheek, and though she tried not to react as anything but a friend, she couldn't hold back a swift intake of breath at the feel of his lips. She knew he'd heard it by the way his hand found her waist, ever so quickly, but long enough to leave her tingly where he'd touched her.

Alice was far more outwardly ebullient in her greeting as she gave Mari a kiss on each cheek. "It's so good to see you. I'm sorry I wasn't able to stop by again before today. I've been thinking of you and your back garden the whole time, though, I promise."

"It's nice to see you too," Mari said, smiling as she stepped aside to let Owen's sister in. "Jacob is already here. He's offered to take a stab at the Cooking section."

After Owen, Alice, and Jacob all said hello, Alice scanned the store. Mars was standing and stretching on the counter, his black fur standing up straight along his spine. "You've done so much since the last time I was here. I'm really impressed."

"Thank you," Mari replied. "Although, I'm not sure I've made quite as much progress as I would have if I didn't keep falling down one book-sized rabbit hole after another. Charlie's section on the rock 'n' roll history of Elderflower Island could fill a museum, and I find it all so fascinating that every time I look up, three hours have gone by and I've only dealt with two shelves, because I'm so busy reading."

Just then, Mars hopped off the counter and made a beeline for the open front door, not bothering to greet anyone when nature was clearly calling—as were the scraps of food surely waiting for him outside the pub's kitchen door.

"That's why we're here to help," Jacob said. "I'm going to get stuck in cookbooks and food memoirs now. Any directions you'd like me to follow, or should

I just get on with the way I'd like to see them organized?"

Mari had spent enough time in bookstores over the years, both enjoying them and secretly dreaming of what it would be like to own one, that she had plenty of ideas and opinions about how she wanted her shelves arranged. At the same time, she was always open to learning from other people—especially when they had special knowledge on a topic. "I'd love it if you could set things up the way it feels right for you as a chef."

He looked thrilled. "I'm like a kid in a candy store, getting to play with all these lovely cookbooks. But be sure to let me know if my organization plan doesn't work for you. My feelings won't be hurt."

"Okay, will do."

"And how about I finish putting together the Gardening section," Alice suggested, "then move outside to start weeding the patio garden?"

"That would be great." Mari appreciated the help more than she could ever adequately express. "I'll bring down some of the baked goods I made yesterday so everyone can help themselves when they get hungry. I'll also bring down mugs and tea bags."

It had already occurred to her that setting up a tea station downstairs in the store would be very helpful—for herself and employees, but also for customers. It didn't need to be anything fancy like a full-fledged café, just a pretty table with mugs and tea bags and sugar cubes at no charge. Something to make the store feel like home and encourage customers to stay awhile. And at the rate she was baking, she could also keep it stocked with an array of little cakes.

"I'll come up and help," Owen offered.

So much for not being alone with each other. Not that she was complaining, of course. Being with Owen, even if she couldn't touch or kiss him, was a million times better than not being with him at all.

Once they were in the flat, Owen's eyes widened at the amount of food covering her countertops. "You've been busy."

"Some people take a shower when they're hoping their subconscious will give them an answer to a problem—I bake."

He reached for her hands, pulling her closer. Closer than they should be given how much she longed to be in his arms...and never leave them.

"Tell me what happened yesterday when you called your mother. Why can't she come sooner?"

Last night, after getting off the phone with her stepfather, Mari had sent Owen a short text message letting him know that it would be at least a week before Donna could come and that she'd give him all the details in the morning.

"Her best friend, Eleanor, is in the hospital for an emergency appendectomy," Mari explained. "Mom is taking care of her until Eleanor's daughter can come to stay at the end of the week." Mari sighed. "I didn't feel right about saying anything that might freak out my mom while she was sitting in the waiting room at the hospital. But as soon as she's gotten some rest, I'm going to ask her to come so that we can talk about everything face-to-face."

Owen tugged Mari all the way into his arms. He didn't say anything, just held her.

And it was everything she needed. His warmth. His support. How good he smelled. The heat and hardness of his muscles against her—

Wait. No. She wasn't supposed to let herself go there. Not yet, anyway.

With great reluctance, she drew away from his embrace. "You must be wondering what you've done, getting involved with me."

"If family didn't mean this much to you, I wouldn't have fallen head over heels for you."

If ever there was a cue for a kiss, that was it. Instead, after a heavy moment of staring at each other's lips, they both awkwardly turned to pick up trays, his with cupcakes and hers with lemon bars. He grabbed several mugs through the handles while she put a box of tea bags beneath her arm and picked up the electric kettle.

"What section of the store can I be the most help in today?" he asked when they were heading out of the flat and down the stairs.

"Actually, instead of working on cleaning and organizing today, I'd love it if you could take a look at the business plan I'm putting together. I've finally been through Charlie's books, so I have a fairly good sense of how the business was going. Unfortunately, it won't survive much longer unless I can bring in more revenue. Lots more."

"I'd be happy to look at it. And to brainstorm revenue-generating ideas with you too."

"I'm up for trying anything that will work," she said. "Even if it's a long shot."

"It's going to work, Mari. I know it will. You're too smart and too determined for it not to."

It was almost exactly what her brother had said in his email. And though she still had plenty of daunting hurdles to leap—and every cell in her body was yearning for more of Owen's kisses—his faith in her made it so that she couldn't stop smiling, even after nearly bringing down an entire bookcase of legal books on her head a short while later.

★ ★ ★

Owen was impressed by Mari's business plan. Hugely

so. Though she had been overloaded this week with cleaning and reshelving the books, not to mention her discoveries about Charlie's life and the stories he'd written, she'd also managed to put together one heck of a good plan for the shop. Everything from creating a state-of-the-art website, which her stepbrother had evidently offered to build, to coordinating a multi-pronged social media campaign, to contacting mystery, thriller, romance, literary, and nonfiction reading groups to set up regular book club nights, to supporting local artists with a gallery wall, to reaching out to a list of local publications she hoped would be interested in covering the shop's relaunch, to continuing talks with the TV network execs who had been interested in filming Mathilda's series in the shop.

Just as he'd predicted, she was going to make a success of the shop. There was no way her mother wouldn't be just as impressed as he was once Donna Everett came to Elderflower Island and talked with Mari in person about her daughter's well thought-out plan.

While the four of them took a tea and cupcake break, Alice and Jacob weighed in with additional ideas for the business plan. Alice suggested a twice-a-year plant swap and gardening book sale out in front of the shop. Jacob suggested cooking demos from chefs using both new and old cookbooks. Owen suggested setting up writing workshops and mini-conferences in the shop. Mari was thrilled with everyone's input, and then Alice and Jacob both announced they had to be on their way.

Leaving Owen alone with the woman he wanted now more than ever.

The first day they'd met, he'd been struck by her natural beauty. Her resilience was the next thing to wow him, quickly followed by her intelligence. And now, her utter determination to not only keep the bookshop open, but also to build it into something absolutely remarkable. That she was devoted to family felt like the icing on the cake.

Perfectly whipped, delicious icing that he couldn't yet devour. Which was why there was no way he was going to let them make the mistake of staying alone in the shop together tonight.

"You've been working hard since sunup." It was two o'clock, and she'd already put in a full day's work. "Time for a break."

She looked around the shop. "There's still so much to do."

"Trust me, after you spend some time in the places I'd like to take you, you'll be even more inspired when you return."

"How can I say no to that?" she replied before heading upstairs to grab her things.

Five minutes later, Mari was ready to go, her hair pulled into a ponytail, wearing dust-free black jeans and a sky-blue jumper. "Do I look okay for wherever it is we're going?"

"You look perfect." He nearly forgot his restraint and kissed her. Remembering their agreement at the last second, he walked to the door and held it open for her. "Your chariot to Waterloo Station awaits."

CHAPTER EIGHTEEN

Afterward, Mari couldn't decide which part of the day she'd loved best. Over the course of the afternoon, Owen took her on a whirlwind tour through some of the best literary haunts in London. It was exactly the boost she needed.

They started at the London Library in St. James's Square, where Owen had a membership. Thomas Carlyle founded the library in 1841, and for the past nearly two hundred years, writers such as Agatha Christie, Virginia Woolf, T. S. Eliot, and even Sir Winston Churchill had been members. Mari was hardly able to believe she was walking the same halls, looking at the same shelves of books that Charles Dickens, Sir Laurence Olivier, and Charles Darwin had perused during their lifetimes.

Though she wasn't an author herself, and didn't see herself becoming one anytime soon, she could easily have spent a full day in the London Library, whether looking through the hundred-year-old newspaper archives from *The Times* or the endless array of coffee-table books on every subject imaginable. The fact that this magnificent library was only a thirty-minute ride away on the Tube was yet another huge bonus to staying in England.

Next, they ventured around the corner from the London Library to Fortnum & Mason, one of the world's most impressive and luxurious department stores. Owen treated her to a delicious afternoon tea. Mari wasn't sure why sandwiches tasted so much better when they were small and cut into triangles with the crusts cut off. All she knew was that they did. The freshly baked scones and petits fours for dessert didn't hurt either.

And then they were off again to visit the home of Charles Dickens at 48 Doughty Street, where he'd written *Oliver Twist* and *Nicholas Nickleby*. Again, it was hard to believe that she was actually in the same room where the great author had sat at his writing desk and penned his masterpieces.

Mari had always been enthralled by books, but coming to the country and city where so many of the great works of literature had been written was making her fall in love with books all over again.

Though Owen was close by throughout the afternoon, she got lost in her own world. And he seemed to relish just being there with her, rather than trying to get her attention or engage her in conversation. She was immensely grateful for the chance to simply soak it all in. Later, there would be time to discuss and debate. But for a few precious hours, she let herself be swept up in pure joy and wonder.

By the time they walked out of the Charles Dickens Museum, she was full to the brim with happiness—and gratitude. "Thank you so much for today."

"It's not quite over yet."

"Surely everything is closed by now. And you've already taken me to see so much."

"I know you must be anxious to get back to the shop to dive into your piles of books," he said with a smile, "but there's one more place I'd like to take you tonight."

After he informed her that their final destination for the evening wasn't too far from the Charles Dickens Museum, they stopped at a van on the corner of a small park and bought soft-serve ice cream, or Mr. Whippy, as it was called here. Even vanilla ice cream tasted better in London, she thought with a smile.

If she could have designed a perfect day for herself, it would've been this.

The only thing marring its perfection was their having to go out of their way not to touch or stand too close to try to keep from leading themselves into temptation.

It should have helped that they had been continually surrounded by people on the Tube and in the busy London streets, but Mari found that when you wanted someone as much as she wanted Owen, it didn't matter how many people you were surrounded by. The desperate longing didn't lessen one bit.

Suddenly, Mari realized where Owen's "one more place" was. "We're on Baker Street!"

"We certainly are." Owen grinned, looking pleased with himself. As well he should.

"Visiting 221B Baker Street has been on my bucket list *forever*. I'm the hugest, geekiest Sherlock Holmes fan."

"Who wouldn't be?"

She stood on the sidewalk in front of the famous black door. "I know this is going to make me look like the world's biggest tourist, but I've got to have a picture in front of this." She handed Owen her phone, and as soon as he took some pictures of her grinning in front of the famous door, he stood beside her and took a selfie of the two of them together.

It wasn't until she turned around and saw the CLOSED sign that she realized museum hours were over for the day. She'd already seen and experienced so much, she shouldn't be disappointed. And yet she was, just a little bit.

Just then, the door opened, and a friendly looking woman said, "Owen, it's lovely to see you again. And you must be Mari." The woman motioned for them to come in. "Welcome to the Sherlock Holmes Museum. If you need anything, I'll be behind the desk on the ground floor. Please, enjoy yourselves."

The first two destinations Owen had taken her to had brimmed with rich literary importance. The Sherlock Holmes Museum, by contrast, was pure fun. From trying on a deerstalker cap while holding the pipe to her mouth as she sat by the fireplace, Owen pretending to be Watson as he looked through the magnifying glass in the seat across from her, to laughing at the wax figures on the top floor that had been made to represent characters from the most famous stories, to reading the wonderful fan mail that Sir Arthur Conan Doyle still received to this day from readers around the world.

Mari had thought her heart was as full of joy as it could be. But Owen had managed to give her even more.

So much more that she couldn't stop herself from throwing her arms around him. "I've had the most wonderful day."

"It's been just as good for me."

The heat from his body seeped into hers, his muscles strong, his hold around her waist giving her that breathless feeling again.

Just then, however, her stomach rumbled, breaking

the spell. She should have been grateful for the accidental reminder to step away, but she wasn't. Not when she wanted more than ever to kiss him...and he clearly wanted exactly the same thing.

"Looks like I'd better get some food into you," he said in a low voice that moved over her skin like a caress.

"I can't believe that massive afternoon tea didn't fill me up for the rest of the day."

"You've been working hard all week. I'm sure your body is more than ready to catch up with food and rest."

"I don't think I'll be able to rest again for quite a while, not if I want to well and truly bring the bookstore back to life. Which is yet another reason why this afternoon has been so perfect. If I ever start to feel tired or overwhelmed, all I'll have to do is think back on today."

Before leaving the Sherlock Holmes Museum, they browsed in the gift shop for a few minutes. She couldn't resist buying a teapot in the shape of an antique typewriter. As she was taking the pot to the register to pay for it, she saw the children's books. The Sherlock Holmes mysteries hadn't been written for children, but they were so popular that they had been adapted in every way possible over the years—including into delightful children's stories that left out the gore, but kept the mystery. The illustrations in the books were good, she noted, but not quite as charming or fun as her father's.

That was when it hit her. "Owen, I've just had the craziest idea."

His eyes met hers and she could see her own budding excitement mirrored in them as he said, "I think I've just had the same one."

They left the museum and headed down the street to a Vietnamese restaurant that he said served fantastic *pho*. But though it was one of her favorite things to eat, she could hardly think about food right now.

"How difficult do you think it would be to publish Charlie's stories? Obviously, I have no idea whatsoever what's involved, but I'm willing to do whatever research or work is necessary to make it happen."

"The honest answer?" Owen replied. "I'm not sure. While Mathilda and I have talked about making children's editions of her books, it's never been a top priority." He looked pensive, obviously turning things over inside his head. "Still, I don't know why I didn't think of it earlier. I suppose I was just so surprised that he had written the books, done the illustrations, and made them all about the two of you, to be thinking in practical terms."

As they sat down to look at the menu and place their orders, Mari realized she needed to clarify her earlier comment. "I would never assume that you'd want to be involved as an agent or manager for Charlie's books. I just got excited and wanted to bounce the idea off you."

"Of course I want to be involved. Not only because I want to see you succeed with the shop—the revenue from a good book deal would help—but also because Charlie was a close friend. If only he had let Mathilda or me or any of the book buyers he worked with see them, I'm sure they would have been published long before now."

"I know I shouldn't get my hopes up," she said softly, "but it feels so right, doesn't it? To think that Charlie's books might one day not only be in bookstores, but in *his* bookstore."

"Why shouldn't you get your hopes up? After all, isn't hope what we're holding on to, for the shop and for us, as well? Why not add our hopes about Charlie's stories making the journey from his notebooks to the printed page and to digital readers in people's homes?" He was smiling as he said, "Any other hopes you'd like to add to our list?"

"I hope I never forget how happy I've been today, no matter what happens in the future. And," she added in a soft voice, "I hope you know how much meeting you, spending time with you, talking with you, dreaming with you means to me."

With that, their bowls of food were delivered. Her appetite roared back to life, and she devoured every last morsel of noodles, vegetables, tofu, and aromatic broth while they discussed everything they'd seen today. Owen told her how much he loved the *Frankenstein* book display at the London Library. She told him how inspired she was to reread *A Christmas Carol*, even though it wasn't the holiday season, simply so that she could think of Dickens writing it in the office she'd stood in only hours ago.

According to Owen, they had barely scratched the surface of everything that London, and the rest of what England, Ireland, Scotland, and Wales had to offer, with a new wonder around every corner. All she had to do was get on a train or plane or bus and she could be transported into a world of history and adventure beyond her wildest dreams.

She was struck by a pang of regret that she had waited so long to get on that plane in the first place and take that step into a new world. At last, Mari had to be honest with herself and admit that, deep down, she had stayed in Santa Monica in case her father ever came to find her—because what if the one time she left was when he finally showed up?

Her behavior hadn't been rational by any stretch of the imagination. But love, she was beginning to understand, wasn't always rational. The heart wanted what it wanted.

What she already felt for Owen was imprinted on her soul. No amount of telling her heart to quit or to give up its feelings would make a lick of difference. Which only made it more important that her parents should come around to accepting him in Mari's life.

There had been no word from her mom today. Mari wasn't surprised, given that Donna was caring for Eleanor, but that didn't make the waiting any easier.

By the time they were back on Elderflower Island, Mari couldn't stop yawning.

"Shall I come upstairs and tuck you into bed?" Owen asked.

There was a teasing glint in his eyes, but at the same time, she could see the longing beneath it. The same longing she felt—not for him to tuck her into bed by herself but to join her there.

"I wish you could," she said softly. And then, "Thank you, again, for the best day ever."

"My family is looking forward to seeing you tomorrow at Sunday lunch."

"I'm really looking forward to meeting them, too."

Though she was working hard at restraint, there was no way to keep from walking into his arms and holding on tight. She breathed in his delicious scent and dreamed of a day in the hopefully not too distant future when she could do so much more than hug him good night then watch him leave.

CHAPTER NINETEEN

Owen took Charlie's notebooks with him when he left the shop, letting Mars in to settle down in his spot by the register for the night before closing the door behind him. His grandmother greeted him with a knowing smile when he walked into the cottage.

"I can see from your happy glow that you've had a lovely time with Mari today," Mathilda said. "So there's no need to give me any details. Unless they're particularly juicy ones, that is."

Owen rolled his eyes. His grandmother might write mysteries for a living, but there was nothing she loved more than a good romance. Particularly the *juicy* parts. She'd tried to write a romance herself, she'd once told him, but she'd quickly realized she was much better at murdering people on the page and sending in her fictional sleuths to solve the crime.

"It was a brilliant day," he confirmed. "Unfortunately, however, things aren't quite as simple as I wish they could be."

Mathilda didn't look surprised. "There's no need to

say any more than you're comfortable with, of course, but it's not difficult for me to guess that Mari's family in California might not be thrilled to have her here." When he gave a small nod to indicate that she was on the right track, she gave him a smile of understanding. "I know it may seem difficult to believe this now, but everything is going to work out. I feel it in my bones. It is what I've always felt, which was a big part of why I worked so hard to change Charlie's mind while he was alive. I'm afraid, however, that all of us have a tendency to build up our worries and fears inside our heads until we're paralyzed by them. Promise me you won't let that happen with Mari. I'd much rather that you held tight to hope, no matter what."

"Not to worry, Gran, where Mari is concerned, there's no way I'd ever let myself lose hope." He held up Charlie's notebooks. "I'm going to scan these tonight so that I can get the pages off to publishers first thing in the morning. I'd like to get a deal for them, both to honor Charlie's talent—and also to help Mari with the bookshop's bottom line."

Mathilda's face lit up. "What a wonderful idea. I'd be happy to write a foreword to the books, if you think there would be any interest in that."

"Are you kidding, Gran? Of course there will be interest. I'll be sure to mention it in my email to the publishers."

"How about a cuppa before you get to work?"

"Thanks, but I'd like to scan the stories immediately. If there's any chance of a book deal in the near future, and by *near* I'm talking a matter of days, it will mean a lot for Mari's chances of keeping the bookshop afloat. In fact, instead of bringing her by Mum and Dad's for Sunday roast, it would be so much better if we had lunch in the shop. That way, everyone can pitch in once we've eaten."

"Yet another brilliant idea." Mathilda always knew how to make him feel good. She was the best boss he'd ever had. He had been out of his mind to have lunch with the streaming company that day. "Would you like me to call your mother to make the arrangements?"

"That would be great, Gran." He gathered up the notebooks, then gave her a kiss on the cheek. "See you in the morning."

★ ★ ★

As Mathilda watched her grandson head back into his office, she was ecstatic that he had finally found happiness. And true love.

Mathilda could still remember those heady days when she had fallen for Benedict. She'd been hurrying through the Cecil Court shops in Mayfair—a street that, post-Harry Potter, everyone claimed looked just like Diagon Alley. She'd been too excited about the chance to buy a new book from her favorite author to pay any attention to where she was going and had crashed headlong into Benedict. Even then, she had barely stopped to look up in her haste to lose herself in a wonderful new book.

But Benedict had noticed her. And once she'd finished paying for her book, she'd found him waiting outside. Her heart had skipped a beat, and she'd known that he was the one she was meant to be with.

Perhaps it had to do with the fact that he was holding a newly purchased copy of *A Dance to the Music of Time*. Anyone who liked the work of Anthony Powell couldn't be bad. What's more, Benedict was so delightful to look at. And she was just shallow enough to care.

When she was twenty-one, her parents had already begun to despair that she might forever be on the shelf, perfectly happy to while away her days reading books and her evenings writing stories she wasn't sure what to do with, but knew she had to tell anyway.

With the encouragement of her parents, and after a wonderful courtship that had made her eyes as bright as Mari's were when she looked at Owen, Mathilda and Benedict were married. Nine months later they had Penny.

Though Mathilda continued to write when she had a chance, those chances came few and far between with three more children in rapid succession. She enjoyed raising her children, but it had been extremely difficult to collect her thoughts during so many nearly sleepless nights with them.

It wasn't until she was fifty years old, and her brood were out of the house and living their own lives, that she finally turned her focus to writing in a serious way. By then, she had read countless mysteries. She always kept a book with her—in her bag, by her bedside, in the sitting room, in the kitchen, in the car. By the time she sat down to begin writing the first book in *The Bookshop on the River* series, she had a fairly good idea of the kind of story she wanted to tell.

It helped that she was so inspired by the environment that Charlie had created at Elderflower Island Books. There was nowhere else she could imagine setting her mysteries. And though the main protagonists were a rather close comparison to Charlie and herself—a man and a woman who were the best of friends, and nothing more, but who enjoyed each other's company greatly, especially as they solved the latest murder in their part of the world—she refused to ever say for sure whether or not she had modeled her heroine and hero on the two of them.

Now, all these years later, Charlie's daughter and her grandson had found each other. Mathilda couldn't be more pleased, even if the going was a bit rockier than she would've liked. She suspected Charlie's ex-wife had deep reservations about her daughter's being here and taking on Charlie's legacy. And why wouldn't she, considering it was due to his negligence—and his drinking—that Mari's mother had nearly lost the person most precious to her.

And yet...

There came a time in everyone's life when one had to forgive. When one had to look at the past and accept it for what it was, without letting it continue to rule the future.

Mathilda understood that well, better than any of her children, or grandchildren, would ever suspect. Benedict had been a good man. But not a perfect one. They'd been married ten years when she found out about his affair.

She confronted him, of course. She wasn't a shrinking violet, and she informed him that she was leaving him and planned to file for primary custody of the children, as well. He'd pleaded with her not to leave and vowed never to betray her again.

Mathilda had made the difficult decision not only to believe him, but to move forward without regret, if at all possible. And in the end, against all odds, he'd kept his vow, until he passed away of a heart attack at seventy.

She knew things didn't always work out so well. Look at her granddaughter Fiona. Mathilda didn't trust her snake of a husband one bit. Though she had no proof, she suspected he'd had more than one affair. And were Fiona to find out and confront him, Mathilda very much doubted that any vows Lewis might make about changing his ways would be believable.

Forcefully pushing thoughts of the man who didn't deserve her oldest granddaughter out of her head, Mathilda decided she would go to sleep happy in the knowledge that Owen and Mari had found each other. She, along with everyone else in the family, would help out with the bookshop in whatever ways they could to make sure that Mari was able to stay.

Before heading into her bedroom, Mathilda called her daughter, Penny. "Hello, darling. Owen and I have a suggestion for a slight change to tomorrow's lunch, one we hope you'll agree is a very fine idea indeed."

CHAPTER TWENTY

Mari was looking forward to meeting Owen's family today. She had taken special care with her hair, makeup, and outfit. While she'd lived in jeans, T-shirts, and tennis shoes since arriving, she had brought a few nice things with her. It was nice to put on a dress, ballet flats, some mascara, and a little lipstick. Of course, taking off so many hours today meant she was going to need to work doubly hard in the store this evening.

The buzzer for Mari's flat rang, and after taking one last look at her reflection in the kitchen window, happy that she wasn't covered head to toe in dust for once, she headed downstairs.

She was halfway down when she realized Owen wasn't the only one standing outside. Through the front windows, she could see at least a dozen people. She first recognized Alice, and then realized the man and woman standing beside Owen's sister had to be his parents.

Mari unlocked the door. "Hello, everyone," she said in a cheerful voice that she hoped didn't betray her nerves.

"Owen thought it would be a good idea to surprise you with lunch here, instead of at Mum and Dad's house," Alice announced before anyone else could get a word in. She was holding a big tray of plants and also had a canvas bag slung over her shoulder with a hand shovel peeking out the side. "He thought you could make use of a big work crew for the day. I'm planning to finish turning the garden patio into a thing of beauty."

"I certainly can use a big work crew," Mari agreed. "Please, come inside."

Alice blew her an air kiss as she passed into the store. Owen, who was holding two insulated grocery bags that Mari assumed must contain lunch, moved close enough so that only she could hear him say, "You look beautiful. And I hope this is all right. Everyone wanted to pitch in, but I don't mean to overwhelm you."

"Thank you," she said first, and then, "It *is* a really nice surprise. I never dreamed so many people would want to help."

"Or that they would all be members of my family," he joked.

Though she recognized Jacob and Bernard from the café, Alfie from the pub, and Sue from the Chinese takeaway, she was amazed that the rest of them must be Sullivans.

"Mum, Dad, this is Mari. Mari, these are my parents, Penny and Simon."

"It's absolutely lovely to meet you," Owen's mother said, giving Mari a kiss on each cheek. "You so remind me of your father. I'm terribly sorry about his passing."

"Thank you." Mari was immediately warmed by Penny. She could see her resemblance to her mother, Mathilda, and yet they were clearly very different personalities. While Owen's grandmother had a bit of an edge to her—one that Mari longed to emulate, as she was certain it was at least partly responsible for Mathilda's considerable success—Penny seemed wholly calm and steady. Yet another set of traits Mari would love to possess herself.

"Welcome to Elderflower Island," Simon Sullivan said a moment later. Mari guessed he was in his mid-sixties. Still a strikingly good-looking man, she could see where Owen got his strong chin and piercing blue eyes. Like Owen, he was also carrying two bags stuffed to the gills with food. "I hope it's all right that we've brought a motley crew?"

"It's a wonderful surprise," Mari told him. "Although you don't have to work if you don't want to."

"Of course we want to work. That's what Charlie would have wanted too."

"Mari," Owen interrupted, "this is my brother Malcolm, and you already know Gran."

"Hello, darling." Mathilda gave Mari a kiss on each cheek. "I'll make myself useful bossing everyone around."

Wow, Mari thought as she turned back to Malcolm. Good genes ran in this family in a serious way. While Owen was the only one who made her heart go pitter-patter, she couldn't deny how attractive his brother was. "Hello. It's nice to meet you."

Before she could decide if she should do the double-cheek kiss with Malcom, or shake hands, he held out his hand.

"It's good to meet you too."

Though Alice had said her brother did something fancy in the city, looking at Malcolm in his jeans and sweatshirt, she wouldn't have known as he looked more like a professional athlete than a billionaire. Mari appreciated that he didn't broadcast his success with a fancy watch or a convertible out front.

A few seconds later, another man with features similar to Owen's and Malcolm's came over to say hello. He had a very cute little girl with him. Which meant he had to be Tom.

"Hi, I'm Mari," she said to both of them. And then, focusing solely on the little girl, she said, "I'm so glad you're here today. You're Aria, aren't you?" When she nodded, Mari said, "Do you have a favorite author?"

Aria smiled. "Roald Dahl. My dad has read *all* his books over and over to me, practically a million times!"

"Me too," Mari said with a smile. "One time, when I was reading *Matilda*, I got to the scene where Matilda puts dye in her father's hair tonic, and I laughed so hard that I accidentally snorted milk out my nose."

"Daddy? Did you hear that? Owen's girlfriend snorted milk out her nose!"

Mari hadn't been expecting to hear the words *Owen's girlfriend* today, at least not in reference to herself. She hoped the blush suddenly splashed across her face went unnoticed, though she very much doubted it would, given her pale complexion.

"I snorted ice cream out my nose once," Tom told his daughter.

"I want to snort ice cream out my nose too!" Aria declared. "Promise to make me laugh really, really hard the next time we're having ice cream, okay, Daddy?"

"I promise," he said, then turned his smile to Mari. "I'm Tom, and I really appreciate your taking over Elderflower Island Books. It would have been a massive loss not only for the island, but for this city, to see it close permanently."

"I hear you're considering taking on the island's concert hall?"

He half smiled, half grimaced. "My accountant says it's a terrible idea. I know he's probably right, but I can't seem to give up the dream."

"I know exactly how you feel. I actually *am* an accountant, and I would likely give a client the same advice about this bookstore. Yet, here I am."

"How about if I help you prove your inner accountant wrong today," Tom suggested, "and then if I end up taking the plunge myself, you'll help prove my accountant wrong too?"

"Sounds like a perfect plan," she said.

"Daddy, I want to show you the Lego bookland Charlie and I built last time I was here!"

Mari breathed a sigh of relief that she'd kept the Lego brick structure exactly as she'd found it. That was when she realized Owen was scowling after his brother's retreating back. "What's wrong?"

"He's already half in love with you."

She laughed at the ridiculous thought. "No, he isn't. He was just being polite and making conversation."

"Tom doesn't do polite. That was straight-up flirting. And the fact that Aria likes you too is a clincher."

"Your brother seems really nice. And Aria is adorable. But—" She smiled into his eyes. "He isn't you."

For a moment, she thought he might break their rule about no kissing for the time being—in front of his entire family. Suddenly, however, a beautiful woman burst into the store.

"I'm so sorry I'm late! Traffic was a nightmare." She offered her hand to Mari. "Hello, I'm Fiona, Owen's sister. You must be Charlie's daughter."

Mari was struck by the way every inch of Fiona seemed to be polished, from head to toe. Though she'd claimed to have rushed here, not a hair was out of place, her makeup was perfect, and her clothes, shoes, and bag clearly cost a fortune.

"Yes, I'm Mari. It's so nice to meet you."

"My husband was hoping to make it today, but he had a last-minute meeting to attend."

Owen was frowning again, but this time there was obvious concern behind it. "I'm glad you at least were able to make it, Fi. It's been too long since we've all seen you."

"You know how busy this time of year is for Lewis," she said. "It seems there's always another business event to attend. Last weekend, we were at a house party with a Scottish duke." Before her statement could come across as snobbish, she added, "I'm still coughing up hairballs from the wild animals roaming freely through the vast, freezing halls. I couldn't be happier to spend today in a cozy bookshop."

Alice had said she was concerned about her sister's happiness. Owen clearly seemed to be, as well. But while there was an air of fragility about Fiona, she also seemed extremely nice. Only Malcolm seemed to be holding back a bit, as though he wasn't quite ready to trust Mari yet.

"I'll see if Mum needs help setting out lunch," Fiona said, then disappeared into the store.

"I can't believe your whole family came to help today," Mari said to Owen. "Thank you for asking them. I should probably change out of this dress now that we're having a workday."

"If you need help with buttons or zippers," he offered in a low voice, "you know where to find me." Shivers of desire raced up her spine as he took her hand in his. "But seriously, be sure to let me know if the gang gets to be too much. I'll boot them out."

"On the contrary, I'm not sure I'm ever going to let them leave, especially if they're the kind of workers you and Alice have already proven to be." Her stomach let out a huge growl. "Clearly, I'm also really excited about lunch."

But instead of heading to where the food was being set up on the garden patio, he stroked her cheek with the back of his hand. "You really are breathtakingly beautiful." With obvious reluctance, he drew his hand away.

After going upstairs to change into jeans and a T-shirt, she came back down to find that Owen's family had worked a miracle on the back patio, turning it into the perfect al fresco dining room. Two long folding tables had been unearthed and laid with linens, cutlery, and glassware. Not only that, but the most delicious food was spread across the tables. Roast beef, roast potatoes, Yorkshire pudding, and gravy. *Yum.* Mari's stomach grumbled again in eager anticipation.

Before long, everyone was seated and passing platters of food, while topping up glasses and chatting and laughing. Mari loved being a part of the group, even if she spent more time sitting back to take it all in than chiming in herself. In her fantasies of what life on Elderflower Island might be like, she had never guessed there would be such a tight-knit sense of community. Or that they would all embrace her the way they had.

It was *wonderful*.

Conversation was light and easy. Whenever Charlie was brought up, it wasn't with sadness, but to share funny stories about how he'd liked to spontaneously read aloud from random books, or how he was a great mimic and could imitate voices perfectly. Mari was happy to share how much she loved England so far and how magical her experiences at the London Library, the Charles Dickens Museum, and the Sherlock Holmes Museum had been yesterday. When asked about the best places to visit in Southern California, she shared her favorite destinations. Malcolm even warmed up to her a little as he talked about how much he'd loved his time living in the US.

It wasn't until lunch was over and everyone had helped clear up that Mari directed each person to where she thought they might be the most helpful. Fashion, Art, and Architecture for Fiona. Business for Malcolm. Music and Biographies for Tom. Alice planned to completely redo the plants in the garden, but realized she needed to pick up a few things at the nearby plant nursery first. And Mathilda would be overseeing the lot of them.

Once everyone else had headed back inside, Owen's parents asked to have a private word with Mari.

"Charlie was a good friend," Simon said. "I hope this isn't too intrusive of me, but ever since we learned about you, I've been racking my brain to try to think of any clues we might have missed. Anytime he might have been about to share a secret, but we didn't give him the chance, perhaps?"

To lay his concerns to rest, Mari said, "Please, don't worry about being intrusive. I'm here in large part because I want to know more about my father. I don't know how much Owen, Mathilda, and Alice have told you about what happened, but the short version is that something really bad nearly happened when I was three and he was supposed to be watching me, and my mother subsequently kicked him out of our lives.

Evidently, though, he'd already been planning to leave, because he thought it was for the best. I'm sure you won't be surprised to hear that I don't agree with either of the decisions they made. But since I was too young to let them know what I wanted, and I can't go back and change the past, I want to focus on learning about his life, celebrating who he was. From everything I've heard so far, Charlie was happiest here on Elderflower Island. And I like thinking of him being happy."

"As I'm sure you've been told many times already," Simon said, "Charlie was a very nice man. And I'd like to believe he truly was happy here, but the truth is that there was always something sad lingering beneath his smile. It wasn't hard to guess that it might have to do with the fact that he wouldn't have so much as a drop of alcohol, even in a dessert. And I suppose, looking back, there was always a wistfulness about him as he watched our kids grow up, probably because he saw you in Alice or Fiona. I can't imagine how difficult it must have been to lose you."

"Anything you ever want to know," Penny put in, "we'd be more than happy to answer for you. In fact, I brought some photos of Charlie if you'd like to see them."

"I would." Mari's throat was thick with emotion. "Very much."

Penny took an envelope from her purse. She handed it to Mari. "If you'd rather look at them alone…"

"Actually, I would appreciate it if you could tell me about the pictures."

Penny pulled one out, smiling as she said, "This was taken the day your father opened Elderflower Island Books."

From the clothes and hairstyles, it was clearly the early nineties. Charlie was standing beside the till, the same one still there today, and he looked proud of his new venture. And yet, just as Owen's father had said, there was also a sense of sorrow about him. Of loss that could never be recovered. No matter how much he succeeded in his career, it seemed grief would never be far behind.

At last, this was Mari's chance to ask about something she'd long wanted to know. "Did he have any serious relationships? Or was he alone the whole time that you knew him?"

"He was never truly alone in the sense that he always had friends, and people who cared about him," Penny replied. "But as far as we know, he never dated. We tried to set him up with another friend once, but he was adamant that he wouldn't meet her. It didn't make sense at the time, but now I can guess that he might not have believed he deserved to be happy once he'd walked away from you."

Mari had always been fairly reserved. It took a

while for people to earn her trust, and her brother was really the only one to whom she'd ever poured out her heart until coming to Elderflower Island. But with Owen and his family, it felt perfectly natural to bare her heart. And to admit, "I don't think I ever felt I deserved to be truly happy either. That maybe his leaving was my fault. That if I hadn't ended up in a dangerous position, then maybe Charlie could have gotten help for his addiction, stayed with us, and remained in my life."

"Oh, Mari." Owen's mother held open her arms. "I hope you don't think this is too forward, but I would very much like to give you a hug."

Mari answered not with words but by walking into her arms.

"You were a little girl. Innocent," Penny said. "You weren't responsible for Charlie's choices, so you can let all those worries, all those false beliefs go."

It felt so nice to be held. To be comforted. To feel safe and secure, even while she was on the precipice of the biggest changes in her life. Now, she was even more inspired to do great things on Elderflower Island, just as Charlie had done.

When she stepped out of Penny's arms, Mari said, "If you wouldn't mind leaving the pictures with me, I'd like to look through the rest of them later. Right now, I'm feeling extra energized to get to work."

Owen's father grinned. "I'm great with a hammer, if you've got anything that needs fixing."

"As a matter of fact, I have *plenty* that needs fixing." Mari rattled off a list that started with the sash window on the left side of the store, to a light fixture in the children's area, to a floorboard that popped up whenever she walked over it. She broke off with a laugh. "Sorry, I didn't mean to go overboard."

"The more work you've got for me, the better. I don't get to put my hammer and screwdrivers to use nearly often enough."

As Simon walked off to get his tool belt, Penny said, "Owen mentioned that you're interested in putting on events here. Could I be of any help?"

"I was hoping you'd ask," Mari replied with a smile. "I understand that you put on the exhibitions at the V&A, which sounds like a truly incredible job. I haven't had a chance to visit the museum yet, but I'm really looking forward to it."

"Let's schedule a private tour," Penny said with a smile. "I did help your father with a handful of events over the years, but he was always a little overwhelmed by big groups of people, so putting on special evenings wasn't a focus for him. If you're looking to pack the place, however, I do have a few ideas that I'd like to run past you."

"Packing the place is *exactly* what I'm after," Mari

said. "If it will enable me to run the store profitably, I'll do pretty much anything. Plus, I've found that I quite like having big groups of people around me."

She smiled as she looked through the windows into the bookstore, where everyone was working hard on her behalf. On Charlie's too. Because they all loved him. Regardless of his past or his quirks he had been accepted and supported as an integral part of the Elderflower Island community.

Exactly the way they were all accepting and supporting her.

CHAPTER TWENTY-ONE

Owen appointed himself all-around helper for the day. Even after their large lunch, cleaning and organizing a bookshop was hungry work, so he passed out what was left of Mari's baked goods and made endless cups of tea and coffee. Along the way, he drafted others to work, including Oliver and Jill from the boathouse, and Ezra who had once worked part time for Charlie and happened to be having a drink across the street at the pub.

Between questions about where she wanted certain books or items in the shop, Mari focused on her business plan and spreadsheets. From what he gathered, she'd had a fairly intense but good conversation with his parents after lunch, and he was happy to see that she looked at peace.

By five o'clock, when Owen stopped to assess the group's progress, he was amazed by what he saw. "Mari." He waited until she lifted her head from her computer. "Look at what's happened to your bookshop."

She blinked several times, as though to clear her vision. And then, he saw it on her face. The surprise. The wonder.

The joy.

Elderflower Island Books was now completely changed from the space she'd walked into that first day, straight off the plane from Los Angeles. Not only was everything now clean and in its proper place, but the shop was also much more colorful and inviting than it had been during Charlie's tenure.

Fiona was a genius with interiors. Her home in Chelsea was wasted on her husband. Lewis was always out at some swanky cocktail bar, or on a business trip, and their expensive six-bedroom house was little more than a stopping-over pad for him, though Fiona had worked hard to make it a home for them both. Today, she'd come with her Range Rover jammed full of rugs, lamps, throws, and fabrics. She'd also brought her sewing machine, which she'd used to whip up covers for several cozy but worn armchairs.

Fiona wasn't the only one who had gone above and beyond. Jacob and Bernard had painted the back wall a teal green that mirrored the color of the river outside. Owen's mother had hung traditional British bunting, decorated with colorful illustrations of books. Alice had put her immense garden design skills to use by transforming the back patio into a place where people would happily sip a cup of tea and eat a brownie while enjoying a new book amidst blooming plants. Owen's father had fixed every squeaky floorboard and stuck window sash, along with anything that wasn't perfectly screwed on or centered. Working with his hands was Simon Sullivan's happy place.

Owen loved watching Mari take it all in. He could see how inspired and excited she was about her future. A future that he hoped included him.

If only Mari's mother could see her now, Owen was convinced she wouldn't hesitate to give her daughter her blessing.

"*Oh my God*," Mari said, barely above a whisper. "They've done it. It looks like a real bookstore where customers can come and browse the shelves and buy books." She turned her head left, then right, then left again. "A part of me thought it might never happen—or that if it did, it would take *so* much longer than this." She squeezed his hand, grinning. "Your family, your friends, they're amazing!"

"They're your friends too," he reminded her. Not just friends, but her family, as well. Just as they been Charlie's family.

He went to the register and handed the antique bell to her. "When Charlie wanted to get people's attention, he used this."

She looked at the bell for a moment, then rang it

with purpose. Everyone looked up.

"Sorry to disturb you in such an ear-splitting way," she said with a laugh, "but I wanted you all to know that because of your help and support, I've decided that this Saturday—a little less than one week from today—Elderflower Island Books will open for business again!"

Everyone clapped, and whooped, and cheered. Fortunately, Fiona had thought to bring several bottles of bubbly in a cooler in the back of her Rover, so they popped the corks and toasted each other's hard work. Most of all, they toasted Mari for her bravery and for her determination to continue her father's legacy.

★ ★ ★

Mari was exhausted yet exhilarated at the same time. Everybody had left by now, except for Owen, and Mars the cat was tucked in on the counter for the night. Mari had spent the last ten minutes walking around the store, looking at each different corner and section, appreciating yet again everyone's tremendous work.

Elderflower Island Books looked incredible. It was exactly the kind of space she'd always dreamed of owning.

Only, owning this bookstore wasn't a dream. It wasn't a fantasy. It was *real*. And regardless of how much work she had ahead of her, she wanted to celebrate *now*.

As though he could read her mind—which he probably could, given that her happiness had to be written all over her face—Owen turned on the radio to a station playing swing music from the forties.

He held out a hand. "Dance with me."

Maybe it should have been strange to dance in the middle of a bookstore, but it felt exactly right. Especially when she was in Owen's arms, and they were laughing and twirling together.

She loved everything about being with him. She had from the very beginning. Even when her brain had cautioned her to be wary, her heart had known better. Known that he was someone she could trust. Someone who would never betray her. Someone who would never intentionally let her down. And she wanted to be there for him in every way he needed her too.

She'd believed that they needed to wait until her mother came to England and Mari managed to wring a blessing out of her. But only now did she realize the truth.

It had been her *own* fears holding her back. Her fears that she couldn't trust her feelings for Owen because maybe, just maybe, her mother was right about charming Englishmen blowing her hopes and dreams to smithereens. Her fears that she might not be enough for him, because she'd mistakenly believed she hadn't been enough for her father to stay. Her fears that she wouldn't be able to hack it in England and would end up back in California, with her secret dreams still buried deep.

But Mari wasn't afraid anymore.

"I don't want to wait." Her voice was determined. And full of desire. "I want to be with you. Tonight."

"I want that too." He pulled her closer. Though the music was still going, they were no longer dancing. They were simply holding each other tightly. "But we agreed to wait so that you wouldn't risk losing your relationship with your mother."

"There's always a risk to everything we do," she said. "That's what I've finally realized. Coming here. Revitalizing the store. Falling for you. Every last thing I've done since leaving California has been a risk. Risks I'm glad I've been brave enough to take with no guarantees that things will work out, or that everyone will end up happy." She moved closer to the man she'd fallen for. "All I know is that when I'm with you, I'm happy. And I'm willing to risk it all. To risk *everything* for you. For *us*."

"Are you sure?" She could see the conflict in his face. How badly he wanted her—and also how much he *didn't* want to drive a wedge between her and her family. "I'd never forgive myself if I pushed you too fast, or lost you because I couldn't be patient."

His concern for her only made Mari more certain.

"I've never been more sure about anything in my whole life than I am about being with you tonight. I can't predict or control what my mother is going to do, if she's even going to agree to come here, or what she's going to say if she does. But I can tell you with one hundred percent of my heart that what I feel for you is the most real, most wonderful thing I've ever felt in my life." She lifted her hand to his beautiful face. "Come upstairs with me, Owen. Come upstairs and *stay*."

He took her hand and led her up to the flat.

CHAPTER TWENTY-TWO

Owen stood in Mari's bedroom, holding her hands in his. "You're so beautiful."

She smiled, and it was as though sunlight came streaming through the windows, despite the clouds outside. "I really do feel beautiful when I'm with you. It's the way you look at me." She looked down at her hands in his. "The way you touch me."

He lifted her hands to his lips and gently kissed the tip of each finger, one at a time. She trembled with need each time his mouth brushed over her skin, and he loved it. Loved knowing that she was held just as much in thrall to him as he was to her.

It was something he'd never felt before. Something that had always been utterly elusive with other women. Something he'd only ever feel for Mari.

Love.

He loved her.

Maybe there were people who would say it was too soon. People who would claim that love had to grow over time. People who would say that the desire he felt for her was confusing his heart.

But Owen knew better. Knew, with perfect certainty, that Mari was the one for him.

She was the one he had been waiting for. She was the one he would fight for. She was the one he would unabashedly and unreservedly declare himself to this very moment. Before he took her to bed. So that she would never think the words had fallen from his lips in the heat of passion.

Just as she'd said, life was a series of risks. And this was a risk he would happily take a million times over. The risk of giving her his heart, even without the certainty that she'd give hers back.

"I love you." He brushed the pad of his thumb over her lower lip, and when she trembled again, his smile widened. "I'm not expecting you to say it back to me tonight. I simply need you to know how I feel."

Though she didn't reply with words, when she wound her arms around his neck and went up on her toes to kiss him, he could feel how deeply she cared in the press of her lips against his.

She felt positively gorgeous, and he couldn't resist sliding his hands from hers to run them over her lithe curves. *Finally.* Alone in his bed this week, he'd been unable to sleep while thinking of her just down the lane. So close yet so far.

The reality of being with Mari, however, was a million times better than his fantasies. The heat of her skin, her enticing scent, her sounds of pleasure as their kisses deepened. She tasted so sweet, and he grew more addicted to her with every nip of her full lips.

"*Owen.*" She shuddered as she whispered his name, her hands grasping at his shoulders as though she needed to hold tightly to him to stay upright.

He lifted her into his arms, walked to the bed, then lay her down across it. For a moment, he simply drank her in with his gaze. The way her soft, auburn hair floated across the pillow. The brightness of her eyes as she looked up at him. The sensuality of her mouth, pink and plump from their passionate kisses.

And when she reached up to pull him down with her, he knew what true happiness was. Not only sharing a bed with Mari—but, if she returned his love, sharing his *life* with her.

* * *

Mari felt like she was floating on air. How many times had she longed to be close to Owen like this? It felt as though she had known him for years, rather than days.

Though she wasn't a virgin, she hadn't been with many men. And as Owen kissed the pulse point on her neck, she realized none of those men had counted. They hadn't even been practice for the real thing.

Nothing could have prepared her for Owen. For

meeting him. For falling for him.

For hearing him say *I love you*.

As though he could read her mind, he said, "I've told you I love you. Now it's time for me to *show* you."

But though she hadn't said the three little words to him yet, she wanted to show him too. Show him the emotions overflowing her heart.

A beat later, she rolled them over in the bed. A flash of surprise lit his features at her strength and agility. "I took four years of karate lessons," she said with a grin.

Before she could feel shy, she reached for his T-shirt and pulled it up. His incredible washboard stomach muscles were revealed as he lifted his arms to help her draw the fabric up over his head.

Oh my. She had to touch him, had to run her palms, her fingertips, over his gloriously tanned skin, his muscles rippling beneath her touch. "I thought it was impossible to get a tan in England."

"Any hint of sun and I'm guilty of whipping off my shirt in Gran's garden, even in the middle of a workday."

She could feel his heart beating fast and strong beneath her hand. "I'll have to remember to stop by whenever the sun peeks through."

And then she was giving in to yet another impossible-to-ignore urge, this time to kiss his bare skin, first his chest and then his flat stomach.

Beneath his jeans, his arousal pressed hard against the zipper. Yet again, she wanted to touch, to kiss. She didn't so much as pause before first laying her hand over his fabric-covered erection, then shifting to kiss the straining denim. She felt him throb once, twice, then a third time as a groan escaped his lips.

She felt bold and desperately excited as she popped the button at the top of his jeans and pulled down the zipper. He helped her slide the denim off, kicking off his shoes and socks at the same time so that he was left wearing only boxers.

Every inch of Owen was physical perfection, from his broad shoulders, to his washboard abs, to his muscular arms and legs. Mari had never been with a man so good-looking. Though she remained straddling him on the bed, she rocked back on her heels, moving slightly away from him instead of closer.

"Mari?" Instantly attuned to her changing mood, he sat up with his back against the headboard so that he could hold her on his lap. "What's wrong?"

Shyness nearly came rushing at her. But then she realized there was no reason to get caught up in nerves and insecurity when only one thing mattered. Not whether he was a ten and she was a six, but that they felt exactly the same way about each other on the inside.

She needed him to know what she hadn't been able to put voice to before. "I love you."

His smile took her breath away…and then his kiss did the very same thing.

There were no more nerves, no more insecurities—nothing but joy and pleasure as Owen's mouth, his hands, were seemingly everywhere.

In a matter of seconds, he pulled off her shirt and jeans, leaving her wearing only a matching red and yellow bra and panty set, printed with the emblem of the royal family. If she'd known they were going to make love today, she wouldn't have worn this. Although on second thought, maybe she would have, if only to feel his laughter rumbling between his chest and hers.

"Don't worry, I won't tell Prince William about your intimate apparel," he said through his laughter.

"You know Prince William?"

He kissed her, another hot brush of his lips against hers. "You didn't hear it from me, but Gran just might be one of his favorite authors."

"Of course she is," she said, as proud of Mathilda as though she were *her* Gran too. "Who wouldn't love her books, whether they're royalty or a normal man and woman like me and you?"

Although there was nothing *normal* about the heat smoldering between them, even as they talked about royal princes and bestselling mystery writers. Mari had never been with anyone where loving and laughter—even about her silly Anglophile undies—felt so natural. Or where she felt so hungry, so needy, so aroused.

She'd never known it was possible to feel this way. For her limbs to be this loose and buttery while her belly fluttered and heat pooled at the tips of her breasts and between her thighs.

"You're anything but normal, Mari." He whispered the words between the kisses he was running over her shoulders, sliding first one bra strap and then the other to the side so that they fell away from her skin. "You're extraordinary."

She was certain that no one had ever thought so before. But after a week in London—a week where she not only didn't turn tail and run at the bumps in the road, but had also found love—Mari was starting to believe that she actually *was* extraordinary.

It struck her that every woman should believe in herself the way she now did. Silently, she vowed to help her customers do that, whether with a book recommendation, by bringing in guest speakers in her store, or by connecting them a group of fellow readers.

"I love you," she said again against his lips.

With every kiss, the heat between them leaped higher, making them both nearly feverish with need by the time they finally drew apart. She wasn't sure who ripped the remaining fabric from her skin—it could have been either of them at that point—only that the feel of Owen's lips and tongue and the light brush of his teeth over her breasts were the most amazing sensations she had ever felt in her life. So good that she couldn't hold back her moans of pleasure.

But there was even more pleasure, more breathless sensation to come, as he slowly kissed his way over her breasts and stomach, his large hands cupping her hips as he lowered his mouth to her sex.

Mari arched up off the bed, giving him everything they were both so desperate for.

Again and again, he tasted her so that the bliss of his hands and tongue and lips on her skin was the only thing she knew. Soon, she couldn't hold her tremors back. Tremors that spun into a soul-shaking earthquake as she catapulted into climax.

She didn't know when he climbed back up her body, only that he was holding her, and stroking her hair, and telling her that he'd never seen anything so beautiful as she was in all his life.

She wanted to give him the same pleasure he'd just given her, but her limbs, her lips, wouldn't obey any command but to wrap herself even more tightly around him.

As he levered up over her, she realized he'd already put on protection. Beyond thankful that she didn't need to wait one more second to make him hers, she gained control of herself enough to roll them again so that his back was on the bed—then she took him inside with one thrust of her hips against his.

"*Owen.*" She stilled over him as pure joy washed through her. She wanted to remember this moment forever, wanted to imprint it on her brain and heart. But there was no stopping the instinctive roll of her hips against his at the same moment that he thrust even harder into her.

They reached for each other's hands, their fingers threading together as they drove each other higher and higher. Needing to kiss him, she leaned forward, their hands entwined above their heads as their bodies sped toward bliss.

And as he groaned her name against her lips, his deep pleasure spinning hers out a second time, Mari could feel the love flowing from his heart to hers and back again.

At last, though much in her life remained uncertain, she finally knew peace and unconditional love in Owen Sullivan's arms.

CHAPTER TWENTY-THREE

Owen woke the next morning to find Mari standing beside the bed, holding two cups of coffee, steam rising from the mugs.

"Good morning." Light was streaming in over her smiling face. "I know we've always had tea together before, but coffee is my first drink of the day."

"Mine too." He took both mugs from her and put them on the bedside table, then drew her down with him to the bed so that she was cuddled into the space between his legs, her back pressed to his chest. He handed her a mug and took the other for himself. "I can't think of a more perfect way to start the day."

She took a sip. Then said, "I can." Her voice had pitched slightly lower. A little husky. Just as it had when she'd asked him to come upstairs with her last night. "Come take a bath with me."

"There isn't one single thing I'd like to do more."

They put their mugs back on the side table, but before they got out of bed, she turned to kiss him. Her kiss was soft and sweet, but no less powerful for its gentleness. Though she wasn't the kind of woman to raise her voice or push her way to the front of a line, Mari's passions ran deep.

And she stirred Owen's soul in a way no one else ever had.

Slowly, she drew back. "I could kiss you all day and never want to stop."

Of course he had to kiss her again, because he felt exactly the same way.

For a few minutes, it looked like they might not make it into the bath. But just as he was about to lay her down in the sheets, she tugged him up. "One of the first fantasies I had about you was in the clawfoot tub."

Pleasure shot through him to know that she'd been fantasizing about him all the while he'd been fantasizing about her. "Tell me more."

Her cheeks had flamed from her sensual admission, but that didn't stop her from saying, "I'd rather show you."

Last night, he'd led her up the stairs. This morning, she led him to the bath.

Mari was wearing a thin silk robe, and it brushed his ankles as it fluttered behind her while they walked into the bathroom. He couldn't wait to strip the silk from her body, with its curves and hollows that felt as though they had been made only for him. The robe slipped off one shoulder as she bent to turn on the taps.

Focused on getting the temperature right, she didn't seem at all aware of her incredible allure. Which, of course, was one of the many reasons she was so desirable.

Owen had been with too many women who treated life like one continual photo shoot, with every situation another reason to strike a pose. Mari, on the other hand, clearly never thought anyone was watching her, and had no idea that her natural beauty captured attention wherever she went. Owen would never tire of looking at her. Never tire of holding her. Never tire of talking with her.

And he certainly would never tire of wrapping one hand around her waist from the back, then bending his head to press a kiss to her bare shoulder.

Feeling her shudder of arousal against him, he ran kisses up the sensitive skin at the side of her neck to her earlobe. As he bit down lightly, he loved hearing her soft gasp of pleasure.

"The water's warm now." Her words trembled slightly, as though she could barely get them out when he was kissing her this way.

"In that case," he said in a low voice, "let's get you out of your robe."

Still standing behind her, he reached for the silk belt at her waist and untied it, teasing both of them with his unhurried movements. Though a part of him wanted to tear the fabric from her skin, he also wanted to savor the anticipation of just how gorgeous she would be when her naked body was uncovered one inch at a time.

At last, the tie was undone and the silk fell open. Using every ounce of his self-control, he slowly ran his hands over her bare curves. From the soft swell of her breasts, to the indentation of her waist, to the flare of her hips, and then, at last, to the vee between her thighs.

Her head fell back against his shoulder as he cupped her sex, then slid one finger inside her slick heat as his other hand caressed her bare breasts.

"Mari."

His breath shook in his lungs as he touched her. Owen had never needed anyone as much as he needed her. Never wanted to hear a woman's cries of passion, of pleasure, the way he wanted to hear and feel Mari come apart for him. Right here. Right now. Standing at the side of the tub, with her robe half on, half off.

Adding another finger, he slid deep, and that was when she crashed into a heady climax in his arms. He rode the waves with her, stroking her, urging her on with heated whispers.

At last, they stood together, neither of them speaking, both of them breathing hard. Until Mari stepped into the tub and held out her hands. Together, they sank into the water so that they faced each other, their backs against the porcelain, her legs splayed around his hips.

Her gaze roved his face. "Coming here, coming to England, to this store and flat—you're the very last person I ever thought I'd find."

"And now that you have?"

"If I had known you were here on Elderflower Island, I would have come years ago."

"Which is why we're not going to waste any time now," he said softly.

"Definitely not," she agreed. As if to prove the truth of her words, she floated forward so that she was sitting on his lap, clasped her arms around his shoulders, and kissed him.

It was impossible to keep from rocking his erection into her. Fortunately, she had thought to bring protection into the bathroom and was soon ripping open a condom packet.

Her hands weren't quite steady as she slid it onto him, but neither were his as he gripped her hips and brought her up over him. Every moment with Mari, every kiss, every time they made love, felt brand new. Brilliantly exciting. And when he lowered her so that she could take him deep, both of them lost their breath as pleasure filled them up in its place.

"*Mari.*" He couldn't stop saying her name. Over

and over and over again as they loved each other with such intensity that the water nearly sloshed over the sides of the tub. Lifting his hands from her hips, he threaded his fingers into her hair and kissed her with all the love in his heart.

Together, they flew, soared, leaped over the edge of pleasure, before landing safely in each other's arms.

* * *

Mari's phone rang as they were stepping out of the tub. He saw her tense at the ring tone, felt it in her muscles as he gently rubbed a towel over her skin.

"If it's your mother," he said softly, "everything is going to be fine." He wouldn't let things go any other way, even if he had to spend hours on his knees begging her family to see the situation in a better light.

Mari let out a long breath and nodded. "I know it will be. Because I'm not going to change my mind, and she'll have to accept that. I just hope we don't end up battling one another to get to that point, because I can't stand the thought of fighting with her. Not when I know how much she loves me and truly does want the best for me...even if the things she thinks are best aren't necessarily the ones that I do."

"As my father always says, there's no need to borrow trouble. First, let's get her here. And then we'll deal with her reaction once we see what it is."

"*We.*" Her shoulders fell back to a more relaxed position as she smiled at him. "That's a lovely word. And it's even lovelier to know that I'm not in this alone."

"You're anything but alone, Mari. Me, my family, your new friends—everyone on Elderflower Island is behind you."

Her smile grew. "I really do want my parents to meet all of you. I don't see how it's possible that they wouldn't like everyone as much as I do." She wrapped the towel tightly around herself. "It's nearly midnight in California. I'd better call her back before she goes to sleep." Just then, his cell phone rang too.

"I'm just a text away," he reminded her, though he knew Mari could handle anything life threw at her. With one more kiss, he went to pull his clothes on so that he could head back to his office at Gran's cottage.

★ ★ ★

As soon as Owen left, Mari made the call. "Hi, Mom. How are you doing?"

"Just wonderful, now that we're finally able to speak with one another! But poor Eleanor. Finding out her appendix was about to burst was quite a shock. I'm glad I was able to be there for her."

"I wish I could have helped too," Mari said.

"I know you do, and I gave her your love. She

asked about your trip to England." Her mother's tone changed slightly—less open, with definite undertones of worry. "But I didn't have many details to give her, other than from the one phone call and email you sent a few days ago. You mentioned having some adventures." There was an unmistakable edge of wariness in her mother's voice now. "I'm curious what you might be referring to."

"Actually, instead of simply telling you about my experiences here, I'd love to show you in person. Once Eleanor's daughter comes to stay with her on Friday, do you think you and Dad could fly here? I'd be more than happy to buy you both tickets."

Her mother's silence went on for long enough that Mari almost thought the call had been disconnected. Finally, Donna spoke in a shell-shocked voice. "You want us to come to London?"

"Yes. To Elderflower Island and the bookstore."

"Why?"

"It would mean a lot to me if you could see the work I've done. And meet my new friends." Especially one very special friend who had only just left her bed...and bathtub.

"Well," her mother said, "I certainly hadn't planned on a trip to Europe, and I know your father is very busy with work. Surely you'll be finished doing whatever it is you're doing with the store and flat soon?"

"The work has been going very well," Mari said. "But there's no way I can adequately describe everything to you over the phone. Whereas if you came and saw the store and the island for yourself and met everyone—"

"Then what would happen?" her mother cut in to ask.

Mari knew better than to explain things over the phone. Or to say, *Then you would understand why I'm going to stay in London.* Instead, she said, "Please come. Once you're here, I promise we'll talk, and I'll answer all of your questions."

Again, her mother was silent for a long while. Finally, she said, "I'll ask your father if he can leave the office on such short notice. There would be no need to buy us tickets, of course. You know Gary has plenty of miles we can use. If he is free, I suppose we could fly out Friday night."

Which would get them into London Heathrow on Saturday. Right in the middle of Mari's big store relaunch. "That would be amazing. It's going to be so wonderful to see you both again. I know it's only been a week, but I've missed you."

"I've missed you too. I wish I wasn't dead on my feet right now so that we could talk longer. I just hope you never forget how much I love you, Mari."

"Never. I love you too, Mom."

Once they disconnected, Mari immediately made another call, this time to her brother. He didn't pick up, so she left him a message. "Carson, hi. Sorry to call so late, and you know I wouldn't ask you for such a huge favor if I weren't desperate, but if there's any way you can come to England by Saturday, if at all possible, that would be amazing. I've asked Mom and Dad to fly in that day, and it would help to have your support, live and in the flesh, when I let them know face-to-face that not only am I staying...but I've also fallen in love with the man who has been by my side, helping me from practically the first moment I set foot on the island." Figuring that was more than enough bombshells to toss her brother's way in one voicemail, she wrapped up her message with, "I'll explain more when you call back. Just know that I've never been happier."

When she hung up the phone and looked down at herself, she was surprised to see that she was still wearing only a towel. It was time to get dressed and back to the job of making sure her store truly was ready to open by Saturday.

Mari smiled. The first day she'd arrived on the island and seen the state of Elderflower Island Books, she'd been hugely overwhelmed.

Now, she couldn't wait to tackle whatever challenges awaited her.

CHAPTER TWENTY-FOUR

Giving herself only one week until the official reopening was borderline crazy. Then again, Mari had always thrived on a tight deadline. Whenever they had needed to finish a massive project quickly at the accounting firm, Mari had been happy to take it on. Strangely, she found that the more she had to do and the less time she had to do it in, the more clearheaded she felt while working.

Fortunately, as soon as she started digging into her massive to-do list, she found it was barely different than completing a client project. The big difference, of course, was that this time *her* bottom line was at stake. The thought was partly terrifying—but mostly, she was thrilled by the new future she was creating for herself.

The days flew by as she put together a comprehensive document telling Carson everything she wanted on the store's website, created several social media accounts, made flyers that she posted around town and handed out at stores and restaurants on the island, sent press releases to print and online newspapers with the details for the grand opening, and convinced major book distributors to do rush deliveries of the latest bestsellers and her perennial favorites. She gathered artwork from local artists to hang on the handful of open walls and sell. She got the first three monthly meetings on the calendar for the mystery, romance, and thriller reading groups who had contacted the store in the past with requests to congregate in the space. She also picked up where Charlie had left off with the TV network in negotiating the fees to use the shop in the *Bookshop on the River* series.

Whenever she remembered to take a break, she would pull out one of her father's notebooks to read. His stories never failed to make her smile, and across the dozen books he'd written, there were so many positive life lessons. Lessons about kindness, sharing, being a part of a team. Lessons encouraging a child to keep learning and not to be frightened by new things.

It broke Mari's heart that there was no story about forgiveness. Charlie likely hadn't been able to write about something that he was never able to do for himself in his own life. She wished for the millionth time that he'd been able to forgive himself for his lapse when she was a little girl. How very different the years could have been for both of them.

Every time she read one of Charlie's books, she wondered what was happening with the copies that

Owen had sent to publishers last week. No doubt it was far too soon to hear from any of them, with either good or bad news, but she held out hope that her father's stories would somehow see the light of day. It wasn't about the money—although it would certainly help the bookstore's bottom line. It was about knowing that his imagination and talent would bring joy to others, in the same way his books were bringing such joy to her.

Though she was working so hard each day that she should be falling into bed exhausted at night, on the contrary, she had more than enough energy for Owen's incredible lovemaking, which left her breathless just thinking about it.

But there was one very special part of the store that Mari was especially focused on setting up by Saturday's launch. A section that she hadn't let anyone see or help her with—not even Owen. By Friday afternoon, it was finally ready for the big unveiling.

Smiling, she left the store and walked down the lane toward Mathilda's cottage. The weather had alternated all week between rain and cloudy skies. Today, however, the breeze was blowing both the rain and the clouds away. Hopefully, that meant Saturday would be warm, with sun and blue skies and plenty of people on foot on the island.

Mathilda's front garden was awash with blooms. It

smelled divine, and Mari took a moment to appreciate, yet again, how lucky she was to be here. Surrounded by new friends, in a city that felt as though it had opened its arms wide for her. Even the paperwork with the local council and the immigration authorities had been surprisingly seamless. Everyone local she'd worked with had gone out of their way to help her get the approvals she needed to reopen the store under her name, in large part because they'd all liked Charlie so much.

Each day, Mari learned something new about him. That he'd been a brilliant dart player. That there wasn't a trivia quiz he couldn't ace. And that he had been surprisingly good with a needle and thread, often volunteering to help people repair the holes in their heirloom embroideries while he was sitting behind the cash register.

Mari would never have learned these things if she hadn't come to Elderflower Island.

Mathilda waved at her through the window in front of her writing desk. The front door opened a few moments later. "Hello, darling. You're just in time for a cup of tea."

"Actually, I was hoping you might come have it with me in the bookshop." Mari was pleased with how natural it felt to say *bookshop* instead of *bookstore* now.

Mathilda's eyes lit up. "I'd love to. Shall we invite

my grandson?"

As if she needed to ask. "Of course." Mari's smile grew wider, even though it hadn't been too many hours since they'd been in each other's arms.

Mathilda called him, and he appeared with alacrity. "Mari." Both his voice and his expression were filled with warmth. As his grandmother looked on, he drew Mari into his arms and kissed her.

"I was hoping you would come have a tea break with me and your grandmother in the bookshop."

"Of course I will. What can we bring?"

"Just yourselves."

Though it was only a short distance from Mathilda's cottage to the shop, several people stopped to say hello and let Mari know how excited they were for the grand reopening tomorrow.

"Everyone is so supportive," she said. "So why do I have butterflies flying around inside my stomach?"

Mathilda patted her arm. "Anything worth being proud of is worth a few butterflies. Every time I release a new book, I feel the same way—just that tiny bit nervous about whether or not everyone will love it."

If the great Mathilda Westcott could suffer an attack of nerves over her books, Mari supposed it was perfectly normal that she'd be nervous about her new venture. At this precise moment, however, all she cared about was how the two people walking into the shop with her would react to her surprise.

Mathilda stopped at the front door. "The shop looks marvelous, Mari. You've made a world of difference. I hope you're pleased with what you've accomplished."

"I am, thanks to you, Owen, and everyone else who pitched in to help." The bookshop wasn't perfect, but it was *hers*. And that would never stop giving her a thrill. No question about it, though she had enjoyed her job at her stepfather's firm, she much preferred the title *bookshop proprietress* to *accountant*. "If you can wait another few minutes for tea, there's something I'd like you to see, Mathilda."

Mathilda raised an eyebrow. "I do hope you haven't gone out of your way on my behalf."

"Of course I have," Mari said with a grin. "I just hope you like it."

With that, she slid open the curtains in the left rear corner of the shop and revealed her surprise.

Mathilda gasped. "It's perfect! Exactly as I imagined it."

Gazing about the space in wonder, Owen's grandmother explored Mari's re-creation of the living room where Camilla Fernsby, Mathilda's sleuth from the *Bookshop on the River* series, pored over clues. Mari had taken exhaustive notes on the descriptions of the space throughout each book in the series, then built the space to what she hoped matched the picture in Mathilda's head. Of course, it came complete with a full set of Mathilda's books on display, including one in every one of the fifty languages in which the books had been printed.

"You're incredible." Owen drew Mari into the circle of his arms. "Even if you'd had time for this project, I would be blown away by what you've created—but I know how busy you've been this week. I can't imagine when you might have found the time to put this together."

She smiled, feeling happier than she could ever remember as Mathilda settled herself in the armchair covered with the duck-printed fabric described in her books, and picked up the leather-bound notebook and bright green pen that Camilla Fernsby always used.

Several minutes later, Mathilda came over and hugged Mari. "What a wonderful woman you are to bring me such delight. I know my readers will adore the space, as well. Thank you, darling, from the bottom of my heart."

"You're so welcome. And speaking of your fans, I was hoping you would allow me to put together a book of reader letters from around the world. I loved looking through the fan mail in the Sherlock Holmes Museum, and I know your fans would feel the same way."

"We also have some really interesting memorabilia for the series from places like Japan and Argentina," Owen put in.

Mari's eyes lit up at his suggestion. "If you have enough to display, I wonder if we could create a small addition to the building on the right side as a museum for your brilliant work as an author, Mathilda?"

"Well, I don't know that my writing warrants museum space, but whatever your plans, I'm certainly happy to go along with them."

"And as a bonus," Owen said, "I'm sure the TV network will be thrilled that the work of building the set is already done."

Mari hadn't thought of that, but she supposed that was now a point in her favor as they wound down negotiations for the TV deal.

"Come over to one of the café tables I've set up in the patio garden, and I'll make everyone tea," she said. She'd also baked plenty of lemon bars, knowing they would keep well for her launch tomorrow.

Once they were seated, Owen said, "I was just about to come find you, Mari. You too, Gran. I've just received news I think you'll both be extremely interested in."

"Is it what I'm thinking it might be…?" Mathilda said.

Owen was clearly able to read his grandmother's

mind as he nodded, then turned to Mari. "The UK's biggest, and best, children's publisher has put in a preemptive offer on Charlie's books. That means, in theory, that the amount they're offering is high enough that they hope you won't go looking for bids from other publishers."

Mari's breath suddenly felt a little ragged inside her chest. "What is the offer?"

The figure he named was so large Mari had to ask him to repeat it.

Once he had, Mari didn't only have trouble breathing, she was also fairly certain her heart had stopped beating. She opened her mouth, but nothing came out.

"Normally," Mathilda said, "I'm not a fan of preempts, as an auction can often get a higher advance. However, I know the owner of this publishing house quite well, and with an advance of that size, I'm confident they intend to put the full weight of their marketing, sales, subrights, translation, audio, and publishing teams behind Charlie's books."

Subrights? Translations? Audio? Mari's head spun. Earlier this week, she would have happily paid to print the books herself to have a few copies to hand-sell from the shop.

"If you were interested in pursuing this offer," Owen said, "I would work with our solicitors to negotiate the contract. I want to make sure we get the best possible terms."

"My grandson *always* gets the best terms," Mathilda noted with satisfaction.

"I would also," Owen added, "obviously, forfeit my percentage of royalties for the deal so that you get the maximum possible amount to help run, and keep improving, the shop."

Mathilda nodded her approval. "And I will make sure that the payment for writing the foreword to each book also goes to you and the shop, Mari."

"No." Mari gave two shakes of her head, one intended for each of them. "I couldn't let either of you do that. Charlie would want you to be paid for your work."

"He would also want to know that the bookshop he left you was thriving," Owen said. "And with this kind of seed money, there would be no stopping you from putting any and all of your brilliant plans into place—even the museum add-on you just mentioned."

"First," Mari said as she worked to collect her stunned, yet racing, thoughts, "thank you so much, Owen, for putting Charlie's work out to the publisher. And thank you, Mathilda, for offering to write the foreword to each book. Though I know Charlie's books are great, I also know the publisher has only been willing to make an offer of this magnitude because they trust both of you. And second, given that you both seem to think it's a great offer—and frankly, the money is mind-blowing to me—I'm willing to accept it."

"Fantastic." Owen took a bag from beneath the table that she hadn't noticed on the walk over from the cottage. "As I thought we might be in a celebratory mood, I brought some bubbly."

Mari was surprised when he produced a bottle of champagne with a label that read *Sullivan Winery*.

"My cousin Marcus runs a winery in Napa Valley with his wife, Nicola," Owen explained. "You probably know her as the singer Nico."

Yet again, Mari was nearly stunned speechless. "Your cousin is married to *Nico*, the pop star?"

"She's a lovely woman," Mathilda said. "Not at all like the tabloids made her out to be. Same goes for all the other celebrities in the family. They're as nice as can be."

"How many celebrities *are* there in your family?"

"Loads." Owen grinned. "You'll meet them all soon enough. But for now—" He popped the cork, then poured champagne into a new set of mugs. "To you and your bookshop and to Charlie and his books."

Mari heart was full to the brim as she clinked her mug with theirs. However tomorrow went—both with regard to the reopening and her mother's reaction to her new life and plans—she would never forget how happy she was right now.

CHAPTER TWENTY-FIVE

Owen was one hundred percent certain that Mari was going to make a success of the bookshop. Though the only contact she'd had with her mother was a text confirming Donna and Gary's flight details, he felt wholly confident that Mari would be able to work things out with her family, as well. Anyone who loved her would support her dreams. He refused to consider any other outcome. Her parents would be arriving at Heathrow at noon and heading straight to Elderflower Island, at which point Mari would be able to talk everything over with them and have her lingering worries put to rest.

Just as he had all week, he'd slept over at her flat. When he woke at six thirty, Mari was already out of bed. She wasn't in the bath or the kitchen. Which meant she must already be downstairs.

From his perspective, everything was done and ready for the reopening. She clearly didn't feel the same way, though. Every time she gave the space another once-over, she found something new to tweak.

Pulling on a pair of jeans and a T-shirt, he headed downstairs. Halfway to the shop floor, he realized Mari was talking with someone.

"What do you think, Mars?" She stroked the cat, who was sitting on her lap for what Owen was pretty sure was the first time. Almost as though Mars knew she needed extra support today. "Do you think we're ready for customers?"

The cat purred. Loud and long. Then rolled to his back so that Mari could rub his belly.

Mari laughed. "I agree. We're ready."

"You are."

Mari looked up and smiled when she spotted him on the stairs. "How long have you been listening?"

"Long enough to put in my vote of agreement."

Eyeing Owen, the cat gave a twitch of his tail, then hopped off her lap and headed for the door. Mari let him out, then turned back into Owen's arms.

"How are you feeling?"

She took a breath, blew it out. "Nervous. But good." She threaded her fingers through his. "Whatever happens today, I know I've done my best. And I'm happy with it."

"You should be happy. People who used to come to the shop are going to love the way you've preserved the essence of what Charlie created here while incorporating your unique changes. And people who are coming in for the first time are not only going to want to buy more books than they can carry home, they'll also want to come back again and again."

"Has anyone ever told you that you're brilliant at giving pep talks?"

"What about pep kisses?" He was lowering his mouth to hers when the door opened.

"Good morning, lovebirds!" Alice grinned as she handed over a bag. "I've got freshly baked apple cinnamon muffins. I was hoping to get a chance to give the patio garden a quick shine before everyone arrives. A little sprinkle of water and some dead-heading, if necessary."

"Go for it," Mari said.

The words were barely out of her mouth when Jacob and Bernard arrived with trays of one-bite breakfast quiches. Sue from the Chinese takeaway was going to bring egg rolls at noon. By the time Owen had jumped in and out of the shower, then changed into clean clothes, Jill and Oliver from the boathouse had brought two huge sets of colorful helium balloons, one to tie outside the shop, the other to put inside. And Alfie from the pub had come across with coffee.

The rest of Owen's family rolled in next. Tom had organized a harpist for the morning hours and an acoustic guitarist to play in the afternoon. Malcolm volunteered to run the register while Mari chatted with customers—he'd found the instruction manual online and knew the device inside out. Fiona had brought a half-dozen artful flower arrangements. Owen's mother and father carried in a large cake container. And Mathilda, of course, was queen of her own personal *Bookshop on the River* corner of the shop.

Owen had checked one of her fan message boards last night and found dozens of messages from Mathilda's local readers who had learned of the bookshop's reopening—and their favorite author's role in making it happen—saying that they were planning to come and buy new copies of her books for his grandmother to sign for them. As soon as the first pictures hit the Internet, word would spread like lightning to her fans around the world. They would want to make a special trip to Elderflower Island just to take pictures in the *Bookshop on the River* set Mari had created.

He'd alerted Mari that there might be a swarm of Mathilda Westcott fans descending today and that his family was on high alert to help out in case of potential crowd-control issues.

Already, the shop was a hive of activity and chatter. Mari beamed as each person gave her a hug. She was so grateful for everyone's help—he must have heard her say *thank you* fifty times already. They were all just as grateful for her.

Especially Owen.

* * *

Elderflower Island Books officially reopened for business at ten a.m. By three that afternoon, Malcolm had rung up enough sales to run out of bags. Part of it was down to the incredible support the island locals were giving Mari and the shop, as each person who came in made sure to buy something before leaving. But it was also due to Mathilda's fans coming out in droves to meet their literary hero for the first time in a year.

Mari was thankful she had ordered a dozen extra boxes of Mathilda's books. Granted, she'd thought the copies would last a few months—not that they'd be flying out the door at record speed on her first day. At present, Fiona was restocking the shelves for the fifth time, while Tom and Aria helped keep Mathilda's fans in a happy and orderly line.

It couldn't be going better. The only problem was that Mari's parents hadn't yet arrived. She'd checked their flight details online and knew the plane had arrived on time. She'd sent several texts, but hadn't heard back.

Where were they?

"Mari!"

At the sound of her brother's voice, she turned and

practically ran into his arms, she was so happy to see him. At least, she would have run if she could have made her way through the swarms of customers.

"Carson, I'm so glad you're here."

After giving her a bear hug, he said, "Your store looks incredible! It's night and day from what you showed me when you first arrived." He grinned at her. "I knew you could do it."

"It feels amazing. I've never known it was possible to feel so satisfied...or so tired," she added with a crooked smile. "It was worth every ounce of blood, sweat, and tears, though."

"No kidding. You should be ecstatic." He looked around the store. "Mom and Dad should have gotten here a couple of hours ago, right? How did she react when she saw all this?"

"Actually, they haven't come yet. And neither one is responding to my texts or calls. Their plane landed on time, so it's not that."

"That doesn't sound like them. There must be a reasonable explanation." Obviously sensing her unspoken worries that she had been trying so hard to push away, he added, "We both know Mom has some seriously deep-seated issues with your birth father—but there's no way she'd let that stop her. Not after you specifically called to ask her to come."

"That's exactly what Owen's been saying," Mari

said.

"Owen?" Carson raised an eyebrow. "Is he the man you told me about? The one who's—"

"In love with your sister." Owen moved to Mari's side and held out his hand. "Owen Sullivan. It's great to meet you."

Mari watched Carson size up Owen for a few tense seconds before finally shaking his hand. "It's good to meet you too. Mari mentioned you in an email, but beyond that, I'm afraid I don't know much about you."

"Whatever you want to know, I'm happy to share," Owen said.

Mari instinctively reached for his hand, suddenly nervous that her brother might not like the one person she wanted him to approve of most. Though she couldn't imagine what Carson might disapprove of, in her experience, big brothers tended to be overprotective at the most awkward times.

"What was your relationship with Mari's birth father?" Carson asked. "What do you do for a living? And how the hell did you manage to gain my sister's trust—and her heart—so quickly?"

Mari reeled from her brother's pointed questions. But Owen didn't look the least bit put out.

"Charlie was my friend," Owen said first. "He was a friend to most of us in here. Especially my family." He gestured to the packed bookshop. "There are a good dozen Sullivans in the shop right now, and I'm sure you'll meet all of them over the next couple of hours." With that said, he continued on to Carson's second question. "I manage my grandmother's literary career." He pointed to where Mathilda was holding court with her throngs of fans. "And I honestly have no idea how I managed to convince your sister to trust and love me...just that I'll never stop being thankful that she does."

"You're kind, helpful, encouraging, and honest, for starters," Mari said to Owen. "And it doesn't hurt that I adore your family too." She turned back to her brother. "Seriously, the Sullivans are amazing. You wouldn't believe how much they've done to help me." Alice was within reach, so Mari pulled her over. "Alice, this is my brother, Carson. Carson, this is the brilliant and amazing Alice Sullivan, who is responsible for the gorgeous patio garden you'll soon see in the back."

As Alice's and Carson's eyes met, Mari could have sworn she saw a bright spark of electricity arc between them.

"Hello." For the first time, Alice almost looked shy.

"Hi." Carson couldn't stop staring. To the point where Owen was now adopting the overprotective big-brother stance on *his* sister's behalf.

Fortunately, just then Owen's grandmother called him over. Alice was still standing beside Mari, blushing furiously, when suddenly, Mari felt a change in the air. One that had nothing to do with the obvious attraction between her brother and Owen's sister.

CHAPTER TWENTY-SIX

Mari's mouth went dry, just as her palms went damp and her heart began to race.

Somehow, she managed to put on a smile and walk across the shop as though she was perfectly at ease.

"Mom. Dad." She gave them each a hug. "It's so good to see you both. Thank you for coming."

"We wouldn't have missed it for the world, honey," her stepfather said. "How fortunate that we were able to make your grand reopening." He turned to Mari's mom. "Don't you agree, sweetheart?"

But Donna looked nowhere near ready to agree to such a sentiment. In fact, she looked as though she'd rather be anywhere but in her ex-husband's former shop.

As her silence continued, Gary picked up the slack. "I'm sorry we're late. Neither of our phones will connect to the British network, and the taxi driver got horribly lost."

"I'm just glad you're finally here," Mari said, though her stomach was clenching tighter and tighter with every moment of continued silence from her mother.

"Why don't you show us around?" her stepfather suggested.

"Of course. You've already seen a little bit of Elderflower Island on the drive in, so you know how lovely it is. Everyone is so friendly here too." She singled people out for her parents. "Jacob and Bernard own the café. Sue owns the Chinese takeaway. Alfie runs the pub. Jill and Oliver manage the boathouse. And then there's the Sullivan family, who have been absolutely lovely and so helpful. Mathilda Westcott is not only the matriarch of the family, but also a bestselling mystery writer. Standing by Mathilda, holding the cup of tea, is her daughter, Penny, and the man next to her is her son-in-law, Simon. And then their five children. Tom is doing crowd control for his grandmother with that little girl, his daughter, Aria. Malcolm is manning the register for me. Fiona is the one by the window putting together a vase of flowers. Alice is talking to Carson. And then there's Owen."

Despite her tightly clenched stomach, Mari smiled as she said his name. As though he knew she needed him—just as he always seemed to know—he excused himself from his grandmother's side and crossed the room to her.

"Owen—" She reached for his hand at the same

moment that he reached for hers. "I'd like you to meet my parents, Donna and Gary Everett."

"Hello." He shook Gary's hand and didn't make a big deal about the fact that Donna didn't extend hers. "It's wonderful to meet both of you. Your daughter is an extraordinary woman. You must be very proud of her. I know I am."

Instead of replying, Donna turned on her heel and bolted out the door.

★ ★ ★

Mari's mother was moving so quickly, heading up the road past the boutiques and the café as though she were planning to make an escape via the bridge, that Mari had to jog to catch up with her.

"Mom, wait!"

It wasn't until her mother reached the gates of the manor house that she finally stopped and sat on one of the benches, dropping her head into her hands.

Mari's heart was galloping in her chest—not just because of the speed with which she'd chased her mom, but because Donna's reaction was even worse than she'd feared. She'd never seen her mother so angry before.

Only, once she was close enough to sit beside her, Mari realized it wasn't anger that had propelled her mother out of the bookshop. It was sorrow. Donna's shoulders were shaking as she sobbed.

"Mom, it's okay. Everything's okay." Mari held her as she broke down. For so long, she'd feared sending her mother into another massive emotional breakdown. And just as she'd known they would, her mother's tears broke her heart to pieces. "Please, let me explain."

At last, Mari's mother lifted her head from her hands and wiped her eyes with her fingertips. "No, *I'm* the one who needs to explain." Her words were ragged when she finally spoke. "My biggest fear was always that Charlie would come back into your life and take you away from me, just like his negligence almost took you away when you were a little girl. I had almost started to believe I was safe from that ever happening—but then, when he died, all my fears came true when you got on that plane. I told Gary, 'She's never coming back.' And you aren't, are you?"

Mari didn't want to lie, but she didn't want to cause her mother more pain either. "I never meant to hurt you by coming here, I swear I didn't. But I couldn't stay away. I had to see where he lived, where he worked—had to learn more about the other half of where *I* came from. And I'd be lying to you if I said that I regret doing any of it. I would give anything to take back the pain my leaving, and deciding to stay in London, has caused you, though. I'm so sorry, Mom. I truly am."

"None of this is your fault." Donna's voice was so clogged with emotion, her words were almost indecipherable. "You don't need to be sorry. I do. All your life, I've tried so hard to take care of you. To shield you from pain. And to guide you toward happiness. But..." Another sob emerged. "I blew it."

"You didn't." It was the last thing Mari had expected to hear her mother say. "I love you, and you know how much I appreciate everything you've done for me."

Her mother was shaking her head. "I held you back. Not just from your father. But from your true calling with books. As soon as I walked into the store, I could see it. Finally see what I've been trying to ignore for so long. You've never looked so happy. As much as I wish otherwise, the truth is that you belong *here*. In *his* store. In *his* country." Donna looked as downcast as Mari had ever seen her. "Not mine."

Mari had been desperate for her mother see how perfectly she fit on Elderflower Island and in the bookshop. And yet, at the same time, she couldn't stand to see her mom so sad. "You've always done what you thought was best for me. And I *have* been happy in California. I liked my job. I liked my friends and my hobbies."

"But you never *loved* any of it, did you? You're so

much happier here, aren't you?"

In her mother's questions, Mari could hear a faint thread of hope that she might still say she wasn't actually happier in England—and that she would sell the shop and flat and go back to Santa Monica. But Mari could no more give her mother false hope than she could stop being true to herself.

All these years, she'd been searching for her place in the world. At last, she'd found it.

"I am happier here," she told her mother, hating that the truth hurt, but knowing it needed to be said anyway. "But had I come to Elderflower Island any earlier in my life, I don't know if that would have been the case. For so long, I've secretly dreamed of what it would be like to live and work here, but I don't honestly think I was ready to actually live my dream before now. If Charlie hadn't passed away—"

"You would still have come," her mother said in a voice full of reluctant acceptance. "I always knew I was going to lose you one day. I should be happy that I got to keep you with me for so long. I'm *trying* to be happy for you." Donna's face crumpled again. "Even though I'm doing a terrible job of it."

"You're doing just fine," Mari said gently. "And you haven't lost me. Yes, I want to live on Elderflower Island now and sell books, but I'll still come back to California to visit as often as I can. And you and Dad can also stay here with me, as often as you like."

Her mother shook her head. Hard. "I can't, honey. I can't stay with you in Charlie's flat. I can't even stay on this island. You don't know how hard it was to step inside his store. Even though he isn't there anymore, and I know from Carson that you've completely redone things, I can still *feel* Charlie in the place. And that's all it takes for the anger, the fear, the helplessness from that horrible day on Third Street to come rushing back."

It was enough that her mom finally understood what was in Mari's heart. It wasn't fair to expect her to be okay with being on her ex-husband's turf overnight—or ever, maybe.

"I know he let you down, Mom," Mari said softly. "He let me down too. But he's still my father. And even though a part of my heart may never stop being angry with him for walking out of my life and never coming back, another part of my heart will always love him." It was so much more than she'd ever admitted to her mother before. She let out a shaky breath as she decided to hold nothing back. "When I was cleaning the shop, I found some notebooks he wrote children's stories in. Stories about me and him, illustrated with characters who look like us. *Playing Conkers with Mars* is one of the books. Now I know for sure that he didn't forget me."

"Is that what you've thought all these years?" Her mother was clearly stunned. "That he forgot you?"

"What else could I have thought when I never heard from him?"

Donna looked like she was going to start sobbing again. "I swear I never meant to make you feel unloved. I'm so sorry, honey. So sorry for everything."

"I don't feel that way anymore," Mari said. "I *know* I'm loved, by so many people. And you don't need to apologize to me for anything. All I truly want is for you to accept the life I've decided to live. Because when I'm here in London, when I'm working in Charlie's bookshop—in *my* bookshop—I'm finally myself. Finally the woman I've always dreamed of being." She paused for a moment before adding, "I also hope you'll one day be able to accept the people I've decided to share my heart with. Not only the women and men of Elderflower Island who have already taken me in as one of their own, but also the wonderful Sullivan family who have gone out of their way to help me at every turn. Especially Owen."

"He's in love with you," her mother said. "I could see it in his face when he looked at you, and I could hear it in his voice when he told us how proud he is of you."

"I love him too." Mari's words came out in a rush. "I know the last thing you want is for me to fall for a charming Englishman. But he's a good man, Mom. The *best* kind of man. If you give him a chance, I know you'll see why I couldn't help but fall for him. Your biggest fear was that I would leave one day. *My* biggest fear is you won't be able to accept the man I love because he reminds you too much of Charlie."

Donna reached for Mari's hands. "I promise I will accept him, regardless of how much he reminds me of your birth father, as long as he always treats you with respect and supports you and loves you with everything he is. Your children too, if you have them one day. He needs to protect them with his life."

Mari smiled. "Owen is the oldest of five. He's a born protector, and one of the reasons I fell in love with him is because of how much he cherishes his brothers and sisters, his parents, and his grandmother." She paused a beat before deciding to add, "I understand if you're not comfortable being inside the shop, but maybe after my reopening party is over, we can all meet at the pub tonight so I can introduce you to everyone?"

Her mother didn't answer for a long moment, long enough that Mari wondered if she had indeed pushed too hard. Finally, Donna nodded. "Of course I will, honey. I'm not going to lie and say that it's going to be easy to meet so many people who were so tightly tied to Charlie. But for you?" She put her hand on Mari's cheek. "For you, I'll do absolutely anything."

CHAPTER TWENTY-SEVEN

The moon was high in the sky by the time Owen and Mari finally left the pub and walked back into the bookshop. Over the course of the evening, Owen's family had, one at a time, snuck back to the shop to clean it up so that Mari wouldn't have yet one more thing to add to her plate. Even Owen, on the pretense of having to wait in a long line at the bar for another round, had gone back to the shop to take care of some speed-hoovering.

They all wanted her memories of her opening day to be good, rather than of slogging through cleanup when she was exhausted and should be soaking in a bath, then getting into bed for a well-earned rest.

Mari was clearly shocked to see the shop so tidy. "When did this happen?"

He tried to feign surprise. "Must have been the cleaning fairies."

She laughed. "Would these fairies happen to be related to you, by any chance?"

He grinned. "You've done so much already, and

with your family arriving today, we didn't want you to feel overloaded." Though they'd been with each other practically the entire day, they hadn't yet had a chance to talk privately. "Speaking of your family, how are you feeling?"

He'd been so worried about Mari when her mother had bolted from the shop just moments after arriving. And when Mari had run after Donna, Owen had been tempted to run after her too. He couldn't stand the thought of anyone hurting Mari, especially her mother. But he'd known that their conversation about Charlie, and Mari's wanting to remain in England, was long overdue. As it turned out, both her brother, Carson, and her stepfather, Gary, agreed with Owen. The three of them had huddled together, getting better acquainted while they waited for the women to reappear.

By the time Mari and her mother finally did walk back up the street, Owen was extremely glad to see that they had their arms around each other. Donna hadn't come back into the shop, choosing instead to go to her hotel off the island for a few hours' rest before meeting with everyone at the pub later that evening. From what he'd been able to gather over the past few hours, her mother, while obviously shell-shocked by Mari's decision to remain in England, looked as though she was trying to be supportive.

"Let's talk upstairs over tea," Mari said as she

locked the door behind them, then took his hand and led them up to the flat.

Together, they made tea, but once they sat on the couch, their steaming cups were forgotten as Mari began to speak.

"First, I'm really, really happy with how well the shop's reopening went today. I know most of the day's success is down to you and your family and my new friends all pulling together. I hope I can sustain even a fraction of the sales in the coming days, weeks, and years. But whatever challenges come, I'm ready to face them."

"Everyone was happy to help," he said, "but you're the one who pulled everyone together. Today, your shop was the hub of the island, a place I know people are going to want to return to again and again—and that they're going to tell their friends about, as well. You deserve every ounce of the success coming your way, Mari." He laid a hand on her cheek. "Just as you deserve to be supported by your family. Your brother and stepfather both seem well on board with your choices, which is great." Owen had overheard Mari offering to consult with her stepfather's accounting company until he could find her replacement, but Gary had told her that while he'd miss her working for him, now that she'd found her true passion, he'd rather have her focus her full attention on the bookshop. "How are you feeling about where things stand with your mother?"

"It's hard knowing she isn't completely happy about my choices," Mari admitted. "The truth is that I don't know if she ever will be, no matter how hard she tries to wrap her head around them. And she is trying. Just coming to London and meeting everyone at the pub is proof of that." Mari let out a breath, as if she was trying let all her worries go too. "I have to be comfortable with knowing that it's finally time for both of us to spread our wings. It likely won't be easy, not for either of us, but I know it will be worth it."

She reached for his hands.

"I would have given up the bookshop. But I would never have given *you* up. From the beginning, I felt as though you could see beyond the walls I always had up where Charlie was concerned. I tried to tell myself it must be my imagination, because how can someone fall in love that quickly? Plus, I told myself that I needed to figure out what I was going to do with the shop first, before I gave in to my feelings for you. But I've never met anyone like you, Owen. Never met a man with such a big heart, a man who also happens to make my *own* heart race like crazy whenever we touch. No matter what I do for a career, or where I live, I know I'll always be happy with you."

He pressed a kiss to her lips, lingering over her

sweetness. "The first moment I saw you standing here in the flat, I knew my life had changed forever. A voice inside my head told me, *'This is the woman you've been waiting for. She's the one.'* Just like you, I tried to tell myself that I couldn't possibly feel the way I did—not when I had my grandmother to take care of, and her business, and such a guilty conscience that I didn't think I deserved to be happy. But then you smiled, and I felt the truth of it *here*." He pressed their hands over his heart. A heart that had never felt fuller or more full of joy. "Cupid's arrow had struck, and every moment I spend with you only confirms what my heart already knew. You're not only the most beautiful woman I've ever met, you're also as beautiful on the inside. And it's because of you that I can finally see all the beauty around me again."

"I love you." Her three softly spoken words touched the deepest parts of his soul. "Your beautiful British accent. Your remarkable brain. And most of all—" She lifted their hands to kiss his chest. "—your enormous heart."

A beat later, she was laughing as he swung her up into his arms and headed for the bedroom. "No one has ever looked prettier in jeans and a T-shirt. Or made me want to tear them off so quickly." He stole a kiss before adding, "How could I not fall head over heels for the woman who wrote the most impressive business plan I've ever seen, who bakes like a champion...and who faces challenges head on with determination and joy?"

Their earlier fatigue forgotten, they tore at each other's clothes. Soon, they were skin to skin, hand to hand, lips to lips, heart to heart.

Every sigh of pleasure was a symphony. Every sinfully sweet caress a gift. And every passionate kiss another chance to express their love.

He stroked her soft skin and luscious curves, drinking in her cries of pleasure. She arched into him, her breath becoming shallow as she tumbled into climax, taking him over the edge with her for every moment of ecstasy.

And a little while later, when they fell asleep in each other's arms, Owen knew he would always be the happiest man alive.

As long as he had Mari.

EPILOGUE

Elderflower Island Books had always been the perfect place for the Sullivan family to converge. It helped that it was directly across from the pub, of course, and Charlie had never minded having the lot of them clogging up his shop. Mari seemed just as happy as her father had been to see them all on a regular basis and was always ready with freshly baked brownies and scones, a cup of tea, and a comfortable chair to sit in.

Malcolm found himself in the shop more and more often these days. It used to be that he rarely left his office in the city before nine in the evening, and then it was on to a cocktail bar or restaurant opening until the wee hours of the morning. But the nonstop work and the glittering dresses and jewels of the women around him had lost their luster.

Some days, he felt like he was simply going through the motions, making the same calls, doing the same business deals, having the same meetings over and over, faking the same smiles. Whereas Owen couldn't stop smiling *real* smiles. His brother and Mari were the real deal, in the same way that Malc's parents were.

Malc had once thought he had that same magic with the woman he'd fallen in love with so many years ago in the States.

Malc hadn't thought about her in years. At least, he'd *tried* not to think about her.

Funny thing about memories, though…it wasn't always easy to hold them at bay. Especially late at night, when he was alone in his fancy apartment, with his fancy view and his expensive glass of wine, wishing he could turn back time and be seventeen again so that he could get things right this time.

He raised a hand in greeting as Owen walked in. His brother headed for the register, where Mari was helping a customer. As soon as she'd bagged up the woman's book and thanked her for stopping in, Owen reached across the counter, threaded his fingers into Mari's hair, and kissed her as though they were alone, rather than surrounded by customers—with Malc looking on.

Good for them. Just because Malcolm hadn't found his own happy ever after didn't mean he wasn't happy that they had found theirs.

Just then, his phone buzzed in his pocket. Pulling it out, he saw that it was a US number. One he didn't recognize, which always made him wonder—and hope, despite knowing better—whether it could possibly be *her*.

He accepted the call, then listened with surprise to what the caller had to say...

★ ★ ★

ABOUT THE AUTHOR

Having sold more than 8 million books, Bella Andre's novels have been #1 bestsellers around the world and have appeared on the *New York Times* and *USA Today* bestseller lists 91 times. She has been the #1 Ranked Author on a top 10 list that included Nora Roberts, JK Rowling, James Patterson and Steven King.

Known for "sensual, empowered stories enveloped in heady romance" (Publishers Weekly), her books have been Cosmopolitan Magazine "Red Hot Reads" twice and have been translated into ten languages. She is a graduate of Stanford University and has won the Award of Excellence in romantic fiction. The Washington Post called her "One of the top writers in America" and she has been featured by Entertainment Weekly, NPR, USA Today, Forbes, The Wall Street Journal, and TIME Magazine.

Bella also writes the *New York Times* bestselling "Four Weddings and a Fiasco" series as Lucy Kevin. Her sweet contemporary romances also include the USA Today bestselling "Walker Island" and "Married in Malibu" series.

If not behind her computer, you can find her reading her favorite authors, hiking, swimming or laughing. Married with two children, Bella splits her time between the Northern California wine country, a log cabin in the Adirondack mountains of upstate New York, and a flat in London overlooking the Thames.

Sign up for Bella's New Release newsletter:
www.bellaandre.com/Newsletter
Join Bella Andre on Facebook:
facebook.com/bellaandrefans
Join Bella Andre's reader group:
bellaandre.com/readergroup
Follow Bella Andre on Instagram:
instagram.com/bellaandrebooks
Follow Bella Andre on Twitter:
twitter.com/bellaandre
Visit Bella's website for her complete booklist:
www.BellaAndre.com

Made in the USA
Coppell, TX
03 May 2020